S0-AWC-040

ERLE STANLEY GARDNER

- Cited by the Guinness Book of World Records as the #1 best-selling writer of all time!

- Author of more than 150 clever, authentic, and sophisticated mystery novels!

- Creator of the amazing Perry Mason, the savvy Della Street, and dynamite detective Paul Drake!

- **THE ONLY AUTHOR WHO OUT-SELLS AGATHA CHRISTIE, HAROLD ROBBINS, BARBARA CARTLAND, AND LOUIS L'AMOUR *COMBINED!***

Why?

Because he writes the best, most fascinating whodunits of all!

You'll want to read every one of them, coming soon from
BALLANTINE BOOKS

Also by Erle Stanley Gardner
Published by Ballantine Books:

THE CASE OF THE BEAUTIFUL BEGGAR

THE CASE OF THE LAZY LOVER

THE CASE OF THE FIERY FINGERS

THE CASE OF THE SHAPELY SHADOW

THE CASE OF THE HAUNTED HUSBAND

THE CASE OF THE GRINNING GORILLA

THE CASE OF THE VAGABOND VIRGIN

THE CASE OF THE RESTLESS REDHEAD

THE CASE OF THE PERJURED PARROT

THE CASE OF THE SUNBATHER'S DIARY

THE CASE OF THE NEGLIGENT NYMPH

THE CASE OF THE GLAMOROUS GHOST

THE CASE OF THE DUBIOUS BRIDEGROOM

THE CASE OF THE LONELY HEIRESS

THE CASE OF THE BURIED CLOCK

THE CASE OF THE DEADLY TOY

The Case of the
Foot-Loose Doll

Erle Stanley Gardner

BALLANTINE BOOKS • NEW YORK

Copyright © 1958 by The Curtis Publishing Company
Copyright © 1958 by Erle Stanley Gardner

An abridged version of this book has been serialized in
The Saturday Evening Post.

All rights reserved under International and Pan-American
Copyright Conventions. Published in the United States by
Ballantine Books, a division of Random House, Inc., New
York, and simultaneously in Canada by Random House of
Canada Limited, Toronto.

ISBN 0-345-31273-2

This edition published by arrangement with
William Morrow & Company, Inc.

Manufactured in the United States of America

First Ballantine Books Edition: December 1983

The Case of
the Foot-Loose Doll

FOREWORD

EVERY once in a while a man comes along with a new idea. Unfortunately many of these men with new ideas are theorists. Their ideas may be sound but they are allowed to remain in the realm of theory for too long a period of incubation, and the egg spoils before the idea hatches.

Once in a blue moon a man comes along who combines a new idea with the executive ability to put it into execution before the period of incubation expires.

My friend, Theodore J. Curphey, M.D., Coroner of Los Angeles County, is such a man.

His idea is to get legal medicine put on a practical plane and made a part of the highly complex civilization of today so that it functions smoothly in a variety of fields.

Dr. Curphey points out that today over 80 per cent of law suits involve personal injuries in which the medical aspects of the cases are the deciding issue of the litigation; that in large centers of population there are far too many deaths involving criminal violence where the autopsies do not take advantage of all of the currently available scientific methods of crime detection. (The result of this is that not only do major crimes frequently escape detection, but in too many instances innocent persons are falsely charged with and convicted of crimes they did not commit.)

There is nothing startling about these basic ideas. The thing that furnishes the element of novelty is the manner in which Dr. Curphey proposes to put some of his plans into execution.

Space is not available to list these methods in detail.

Suffice it to say that Dr. Curphey recognizes the swarming, teeming, heavily populated County of Los Angeles as being one of the best places in the country to demonstrate his ideas.

He accepted an appointment as Coroner of Los Angeles with the deliberate intention of getting the three medical schools in the district to unite with the law schools as well as with the police and sheriffs' departments in planning a constructive program; of bringing legal knowledge and medical knowledge into a practical partnership; establishing an Institute of Legal Medicine; forming advisory committees to study problems dealing with industrial deaths, maternal deaths, deaths from anesthesia, problems concerning the relationship between the coroner's office and the hospitals, and funeral directors and the coroner's office.

Dr. Curphey also wants to have practical training for undergraduate students in the joint field of law and medicine, a better understanding of the possibilities of legal medicine by the investigative officers and a better understanding of police methods and responsibilities by members of the medical profession.

These objectives are highly important, not only to the County of Los Angeles, but as part of a general public awakening to the importance of legal medicine.

There is something in the practical, two-fisted way Dr. Curphey has accepted the challenge of the problems at the Los Angeles Coroner's Office, has outlined his objectives, and gone about realizing those objectives, that indicates executive ability of a high order, added, of course, to highly professional competency in the intricate field of pathology and legal medicine.

So it is with great pleasure that I dedicate this book to my friend:

THEODORE J. CURPHEY, M.D.

—Erle Stanley Gardner

CAST OF CHARACTERS

MILDRED CREST—A bright young stenographer, she was envied by her friends—until she lost her engagement ring and her identity, and gained herself a charge of first-degree murder 1

ROBERT JOINER—An accountant with *savoir-faire*, he was not only the most eligible bachelor in town, but an embezzler on the side 2

FERN DRISCOLL—A tall, chestnut-haired secretary, she started trouble when she fell in love with the boss's son 7

CARL HARROD—An opportunistic insurance investigator, he called blackmail an ugly word—but he practiced it to the letter in collecting information for a scandal magazine 21

PERRY MASON—The rugged criminal lawyer took on a case of misrepresentation for a five-cent fee and wound up getting more surprises than he doled out to his client 25

DELLA STREET—Perry's wary-eyed secretary played with perjury charges when she followed his instructions; her arithmetic came in handy when she purchased ice picks 25

KITTY BAYLOR—A young graduate student with out-standing bone structure, she was unpretentious about her father's millions but positive that a hatpin was an outmoded weapon for a woman 35

NELLIE ELLISTON—A tough, well-shod "wife," she saw much to gain by going a little farther than her husband suggested 61

PAUL DRAKE—The long-limbed, poker-faced detective did much of Perry's paperwork, and the answers he came up with were not always reassuring 82

HARRIMAN BAYLOR—A stocky, bushy-browed executive, Kitty's father did everything in a big way, including filling up a column of *Who's Who;* his arrogance was great, but his fear of a family scandal was greater 89

IRMA KARNES—The bespectacled counter manager at a penny arcade, she was suddenly catapulted into the public eye when she sold six ice picks on a rou-tine night 119

FORRIE BAYLOR—Kitty's wavy-haired and distinguished-looking brother, his test of true love came almost too late 177

1

AT FIFTEEN MINUTES past two o'clock that afternoon, Mildred Crest's world collapsed about her in a wreckage which left her so completely dazed that her mind became numb and her reasoning faculties simply failed to function.

At two o'clock that afternoon Mildred had been one of the happiest young women in the bustling town of Oceanside, California.

The expensive diamond which flashed from the ring finger of her left hand betokened her engagement to Robert Joiner, head accountant at the firm of Pillsbury & Maxwell, the big department store which had branches located in half a dozen southern California cities.

Joiner had arrived in Oceanside something over two years before. He had started in as bookkeeper and his advancement had been rapid. He had a quick, resourceful mind, was instantly adaptable to any new situation, and above all was not afraid of responsibility. He had complete confidence in his own judgment and soon his employers were sharing that confidence.

An entertaining conversationalist and a good hand at keeping the ball rolling at any party, Joiner was a social asset. He was considered by far the most eligible young bachelor in the community.

Mildred's engagement to him had had the effect of a bombshell in social circles, and for three months she had been veritably walking on air.

Then at two-fifteen Mildred had been summoned from her secretarial desk to take a personal call.

She felt certain it was from Robert, and was mildly annoyed because he knew the management frowned on employees accepting personal calls during business hours. Not only did it detract from their efficiency, but it tied up the lines on the switchboard. However, it was like Robert Joiner to push the rules to one side.

His voice held no hint of anything portentous. He sounded as casual and glib as ever.

"Hello, babe! How's the demon secretary?"

"Fine, Bob. Only— You know about calls here. . . . Only urgent matters. . . . I'm sorry—"

"Pay it no heed," Robert interrupted. "That is just an idea of the big brass to emphasize their own importance. And in a way this matter is urgent."

"Yes?" she asked.

"As of this moment," Bob said, "our engagement is annulled, canceled, discontinued, terminated, and re-scinded. You are to keep the diamond ring and any other presents, and I trust, happy memories of a glorious three months."

"Bob, what on earth . . . ? *What* are you saying? What's the matter? What—?"

"The ponies, babe, blame it on the ponies," he said. "You never guessed it, but I happen to be a gambler, and this was a nice gamble. I like to take chances even when they don't work out. Let the other man go through the humdrum routine of an ordinary existence with slow, painful, plodding steps up the ladder of success! I like skyrockets, baby. I like to shoot for the high places, and I like to work fast."

"Bob, but your family. . . ."

"The myth of my wealthy family back East was simply a background to justify what otherwise would doubtless have been considered extravagances on the part of an accountant working on a salary. My system of playing the

2

ponies furnished a lucrative sideline until suddenly something went sour and I'm damned if I know what it was.

"I started by borrowing from company funds and paid back when the system began to pay off. Then I got pretty deep into company funds again and suddenly realized I was up against an audit. There were a couple of suspicious circumstances, matters of sheer carelessness on my part. So I picked up all the loose cash that was lying around, threw the system out of the window and shot the works on a hot tip at Santa Anita today. A few moments ago the goat came in fourth!"

"Robert, is this some sort of a joke?" Mildred demanded. "Is this one of your psychological tests to get people's reactions? Because, if it is, you've upset me for the rest of the afternoon."

"Let's hope it won't be any worse than that," Joiner said jauntily. "I confess that I feel a twinge of conscience about you. You've been a sweet girl, Millie, and a wonderful pal. But realities are realities, and we may as well face them. Even if I am an embezzler with detection inevitable, I have no intention of putting on an act of tearful repentance, facing the contempt of all the dull clods who formerly looked up to me with envious admiration. I have no desire to throw myself on the mercy of the court, to ask for probation, and promise restitution.

"Since discovery is inevitable, I have decided to make my embezzlement worth while. I have taken everything around here that isn't nailed down. I started for the bank with the stated purpose of depositing funds, and from there I made several carefully thought out maneuvers which are going to make my trail very difficult to follow. Frankly, Millie, I'm willing to bet five to one that they can't *ever* put their hands on me.

"I'll be expected back at the office momentarily, and by three o'clock they will wonder what has happened to me. This is just to tell you that, if they should call you during the afternoon, you can tell them very curtly that our engagement has been broken; that you have no knowledge as to my whereabouts and no further interest in my actions.

"Of course, something like this was inevitable sooner or later. I can't see myself cast in the role of a dutiful husband or a fond parent making sacrifices to put brats through college. Frankly, even the last three weeks of our engagement have been a trifle irksome. You have been sweet and I have had a swell time, but essentially, I'm a roamer and I don't want to be tied down—to anyone. So, that's the story, and now, because the minions of the law will be barking on my trail at any moment, I have to hang up. Good-by and good luck!"

The phone clicked.

Somehow Mildred found her way back to her desk.

A sense of loyalty to her employers kept her hammering away at her typewriter until she had finished the important letter on which she was working. When she took the letter in for signature, her white face and trembling hands attracted attention. She said she felt ill and was told to go home for the rest of the day.

All she could think of was getting away for a time. She dreaded having to face the patronizing sympathy of the other girls in the office. She had a few friends who would stand by her loyally, but there were others whose noses had been put out of joint by the announcement of her engagement to Bob, and they would derive too much satisfaction from rubbing it in.

Mildred only wanted to crawl in a hole and pull the hole in after her.

Mildred went at once to the bank. She cashed the pay check she had received the day before, drew out every penny of her savings account, returned to her apartment, bathed, put on her newest traveling outfit.

At four-forty the phone rang. It was the general manager of Pillsbury & Maxwell. He was concerned about Robert Joiner.

Mildred said coldly that she knew nothing of Mr. Joiner's whereabouts, that her engagement had been broken, that she was no longer interested in Mr. Joiner, and then suddenly in the midst of the conversation, found herself crying. After a few choking attempts to carry on the conversation, she had slipped the receiver into place, hoping that the manager would think he had been cut off.

The manager showed his sympathetic understanding by not calling back.

Mildred had no desire for dinner. The thought of meeting someone whom she knew and to whom she might have to make explanations was intolerable.

Now that the blow had fallen, she realized that for the past few weeks there had been something wrong. Looking back, she could recall a hundred things that should have warned her, but she had been too happy, too willing to accept glib explanations at face value.

Robert had never been one to talk of himself. He always kept his association with her on a plane of jaunty superiority. From the beginning she had sensed that he had an intense aversion to having anyone pry into his private affairs. He would volunteer such information as he wished to give, but resented any questions seeking additional information.

She had been so dominated by the man, his poise, his self-assurance, his clever mind, that she had simply drifted along.

Mildred wished now that she had gone directly to her boss that afternoon and told him the whole story. She wished that she had called Pillsbury & Maxwell and told them what had happened.

Because she had not, she now found herself in an impossible situation. The thought of what was bound to happen the next day threw her into a tailspin.

Dimly she realized that her mind was going around in circles, that in her present emotional state she couldn't trust her own decisions. If she could just escape from everything. It was under such circumstances that the mind in a merciful attempt to escape too difficult problems resorted to the defense of amnesia. If she could just sink into amnesia, but she knew she couldn't deliberately induce amnesia.

Mildred slipped on her jacket, picked up her purse, and started for the parking lot. She found her car and started driving inland, driving somewhat aimlessly, not knowing where she was going or what she was going to do.

She remembered a story she had heard about two years before from a friend who liked to tell horror stories. It was about an earthquake he had seen in South America, and a beautiful young girl, the belle of the town, who yielded to panic. She had jumped in her new automobile and taken off down the road, trying to escape the crumbling walls of the buildings and the threat of a rocky avalanche from the mountainside.

A huge crack had opened up, cutting across the road as a gaping chasm. The screaming girl and the new, shiny automobile had plunged into this cleft in the earth. Then, as though it had only been waiting for its human prey, the crack had closed with a grinding, rumbling noise. The earthquake subsided. Where the crack had been was only a pressure ridge of earth and rocks and the crumbled blocks of the paved highway.

Now Mildred almost wished that some terrific earthquake would open up a chasm in the earth directly in front of her car so that she, too, could disappear. Her one desire was to sever all connections with the past, to vanish without a trace. When you had to work to live, however, in these days of social security numbers, driving licenses and income tax returns, vanishing into oblivion was no easy matter.

Then slowly she began to realize she dared not even try to escape from her past life or to disappear. A simple disappearance would only make it appear she had been

6

Bob Joiner's accomplice in his embezzlements, and she must above all protect her reputation for honesty. She did not have to go back and face the music yet, however, and she needed time to build up her defenses against the sneers and laughter on the one hand and pity on the other that were surely awaiting her return to Oceanside.

After a few miles she glanced at her fuel gauge and realized she would need more gasoline. She stopped at a service station at Vista and while the attendant was filling the gas tank she noticed a young woman standing quietly by the side of the gas pumps.

At first Mildred thought she was the wife of the attendant. Then somehow she got the definite impression that something was very wrong. She felt the young woman's eyes on her, studying her discreetly. Then the figure came forward diffidently.

"May I ask where you're going?"

Mildred tried hard to bring her numbed mind to focus on the situation.

"I don't know," she said absently. "I'm just—going."

"Could you give me a ride?"

Mildred said, "I'm sorry, but I'm not going anywhere in particular."

"Neither am I."

Mildred saw a woman of twenty-three or twenty-four, with brown eyes, brown hair, and about her own build. And she fancied she saw desperation and abject misery which indicated a fellow sufferer.

"Get in," Mildred heard herself saying.

"I have a suitcase."

"Put it in."

The attendant filled up the tank, washed the windshield, checked the oil and water.

Mildred gave him her gasoline credit card, signed the charge slip, got in the car, started the motor, and said to the girl beside her, "I'm Mildred Crest."

"Fern Driscoll," the young woman said tonelessly.

7

Abruptly it occurred to Mildred that if she changed her mind again about returning to Oceanside, she might never receive the bill for the gasoline she had just purchased. She braked the car to a stop, put it in reverse and backed up to the service station.

Mildred said to the station attendant, "I'm Mildred Crest. I just signed a charge slip for gasoline. The amount was three dollars and forty cents. Here's the money. Please tear up the charge slip."

She handed the puzzled attendant three dollars and forty cents, stepped on the foot pedal and drove away.

After a few moments she turned to the young woman beside her.

"I'm not good company. I'm not certain where I'm going or what I'm doing. I may drive around awhile and then go back. I may never go back. You'd better get out and get a ride with someone else."

Fern Driscoll shook her head.

Mildred and the hitchhiker rode in silence for miles. Mildred came to the intersection with Highway 395, crossed it, taking the road to Pala.

Fern Driscoll turned and looked at her, her eyebrows raised in silent interrogation.

Mildred Crest, speeding up after the boulevard stop, at first said nothing, then feeling she might be taking undue advantage of the other's misery, turned to her abruptly.

"That's the main north-and-south road from San Diego to San Bernardino, then to Bishop and Reno. Want to get out?"

Fern Driscoll shook her head. "It's night. I'd prefer to go with you wherever you're going. If I do have to get out, I'd prefer to wait at a gasoline station where I can size up the people."

"I've told you I'm not going anywhere," Mildred said.

"That's good enough for me," Fern said.

"I live back there," Mildred ventured, "at Oceanside. I may decide to go back."

"Oceanside? Where's that?" Fern asked.

"On the coast road."

Fern said, "I'm a stranger in these parts. I arrived in San Diego late this afternoon, left within an hour. A nice-looking young man turned out to be a wolf. I was glad to get out of his car. I walked a mile before I came to the gasoline station."

"You live in California?"

"No." ╲

"In the West?"

"No. I'm just a foot-loose doll."

Silence settled between them. Not a relaxed silence of companionship and understanding, but a tense, uneasy silence.

Abruptly the young woman said bitterly, "I've made a mess of my life."

"Who hasn't?" Mildred commented.

Fern Driscoll shook her head. "You're just down in the dumps temporarily. You've had a jolt. *You* haven't burned your bridges. *I've* burned my bridges."

"I'd like to trade places with you," Mildred said.

"Sight unseen?" the other asked.

Mildred nodded.

Again there was a period of silence, then the other said, "Don't tempt me. It couldn't be done, but—well, it's an idea."

They came to Pala.

"Where does that road go?" Fern asked.

"Palomar Mountain," Mildred said. "That's where the big, two-hundred-inch telescope is."

She turned to the left.

"And this?" the hitchhiker asked.

"I don't know for certain," Mildred confessed. "I think it winds around and comes back to Highway 395."

Mildred gave her attention to piloting the car.

The road ran level for a while, then started climbing, and finally became a winding mountain grade.

On a sharp curve the lights penciled across the shoulder of the road and then were blotted out by the black void of a deep canyon.

Mildred heard the other girl's voice saying, "Wouldn't it be fine just to plunge into that blackness? Then nothing could ever catch up with us. We'd leave it all behind. Look, Mildred, are you game to do it?"

"Do what?"

"Drive off the road?"

"Heavens, no!" Mildred said. "You might be maimed, crippled for life. That wouldn't solve anything. That wouldn't—"

Mildred suddenly felt Fern Driscoll lunge against her. Strong hands grappled with the wheel and gave it a twist.

Mildred was caught by surprise. She threw her weight against the wheel, fighting to bring the car back onto the road.

Fern Driscoll gave a shrill, hysterical laugh, braced herself and ripped the wheel from Mildred's grasp.

In that last brief second, when the car seemed to hesitate, Mildred looked out into a terrifying black abyss. Then she felt the front of the car dip sharply downward. Her ears heard a grinding crash of steel on rocks, then she felt herself lifted into the air, felt the car turning over. Above all she could hear that wild, demoniacal laughter, the shrill cacophony of insane hysteria.

The car hit solidly, throwing Mildred against the steering wheel. Then the car rolled on in a crazy zigzag pattern. For a moment it was right side up. Then it keeled over sharply. Mildred heard a thud, like the sound of a ripe melon being smashed with an ax, then the scraping of metal. With a jolt the car came to a stop.

Mildred had a subconscious realization of groping for the ignition switch and then turning the headlights off, of lying there in the darkness, listening to the gurgle of water from the radiator, the trickling of oil from the crankcase. Then there was a permeating odor; the smell of raw gasoline seeping into the car.

Mildred tried the door. The car was all but upside down, the door was hopelessly jammed. But the window on her side had been lowered. By squirming and twisting she was finally able to extricate herself. The gurgling noises ceased. The quiet of the night descended around them. Overhead the stars were steady.

"Fern," Mildred said. "Fern, are you all right?"

There was no answer.

Mildred leaned over and looked down into the car. It was dark and she could not see much.

She felt for her purse and finally found it. There was a book of matches in the purse.

She scraped a match into flame.

She looked, and knew panic and nausea.

The hitchhiker had evidently got the door partially open and had been about halfway out when the car struck that last huge rock.

Mildred shook out the match, threw it away from her, leaned against the side of the wrecked car, and felt as though the last of her strength had drained out of her.

A car went by on the road high above them. Mildred screamed for help and her voice was swallowed up in the silent darkness as a speck of ink is absorbed by blotting paper.

The car whined onward, never pausing for so much as a moment in its snarling progress up the hill.

With a desperate effort Mildred pulled herself together and took stock of the situation. She had been badly shaken. There were one or two very sore places, but no bones were broken. She could feel her heart pounding, but her mind was beginning to function clearly.

She would have to scramble back up to the road, and stop some motorist. There would be authorities to notify.

She looked down at the dark shape of the girl and for

a moment found herself wishing that the situation could have been reversed and that—

The idea struck Mildred with the force of a blow.

After all, why not?

Mildred could take Fern Driscoll's purse. There would be *some* identification in it. She could leave her own purse. The thing that had once been the other girl's head would now furnish no means of identification. Of course, Mildred thought calmly and coolly, there was the question of fingerprints. Would anyone have those, or would they take the prints of a corpse?

What if they did?

Mildred could try it. If it appeared the body was taken for that of Mildred Crest, Mildred could simply keep quiet. Otherwise she could come forward and state that she had found herself wandering around in a dazed condition, not knowing who she was. She knew that such things happened—retrograde amnesia, they called it.

She leaned down in the wreck, looking for Fern's purse. She found it and considered the problem of transferring what money there was in her own purse. If they found her purse without money— Well, why not? It was money for which she had worked hard. She certainly needed all the money she could get. . . . Swiftly she decided to take all the folding money from her purse.

Calmly competent now, her nausea overcome, Mildred made the change.

Again she struck a match as she leaned over to drop her purse by the steering post. The match flared up and burned her fingers. She dropped it, jerking back her hand with an exclamation of pain.

For the tenth part of a second there was a little flame, then a sudden flare of oil brilliance. As the gasoline ignited, Mildred had only time to jump back in horror before the rear end of the car became a blazing inferno.

Mildred clutched Fern Driscoll's purse, scrambled down the canyon out of the way of the flames. She heard tires scream on the road above as a speeding car skidded to a stop.

Mildred scrambled down the last few feet of the steep embankment, came to a rock-strewn stream bed, followed that blindly downhill, the fire lighting her way so she could see where she was going and avoid the branches which would have torn her clothes.

What followed was a nightmare compounded of many nightmares. There was the difficult terrain to be negotiated. As she put distance between herself and the wreck, the light from the fire was abruptly shut off by a jutting promontory. Finally she was stumbling along in darkness.

When she heard the sudden whir of a rattlesnake, it was impossible to place the noise in the darkness. Mildred knew it was only a few feet away, and the whirring was the dry, ominous rustle of death.

Mildred jumped wildly into the darkness, stumbled over a rock, fell face down in a bush, then extricated herself in the haste of blind panic and ran.

After a while, she heard sirens, saw a red glow indicating that the fire of the car had set off a brush fire. She heard fire-fighting apparatus, then finally found a place where she could scramble up to the road.

There were several cars standing there above the wreck. A man with a badge and flashlight was blocking all traffic. People were milling around in confusion.

Mildred picked a kindly-looking old couple, hastily straightened her clothes and smoothed her hair, and went up to them. "May I ride with you?" she asked. "I got out to look at the fire and my family turned back toward Pala. If I can only get to a phone—"

"Oh, but they'll miss you and come back," the woman said.

"I'm afraid not," Mildred observed, finding that her mind had powers of extemporaneous deceit which she hadn't realized. "You see, I was asleep in the back seat, all covered up with a blanket and my head on a pillow.

They stopped the car and went up to look. I woke up, got out and they must have returned and passed me in the darkness. They think I'm still asleep on the back seat and won't know the difference until they get home."

"Where's home?" the woman asked.

"San Diego."

"Well, we're going the other way, to Riverside. Perhaps you'd better notify—"

"Oh, that will be quite all right," Mildred said. "I'll go to Riverside with you and then I can phone my folks. If they aren't home yet, I'll telephone the neighbor. I have friends in Riverside."

So Mildred had gone to Riverside. Then a bus had taken her into Los Angeles. She registered at a downtown hotel as F. Driscoll.

It was late that night when Mildred surveyed the contents of Fern Driscoll's oversized purse. It was then that she began to appreciate her predicament.

In a neat, compact bundle with heavy elastic bands she found forty, crisp, new hundred-dollar bills. In addition, there were some two hundred dollars in fives, tens and twenties. There was a driver's license giving Fern Driscoll's residence as Lansing, Michigan. There was a social security card, lipstick, a handkerchief, a compact, and there was a bundle of letters tightly tied up with waxed thread.

Mildred hesitated a moment, then untied the thread, looked through some of the letters. They were love letters signed by the name "Forrie." They were most affectionate, but they also indicated a family conflict, a father who was putting pressure to bear on his son to make him "come to his senses."

The letters only emphasized Mildred's own heartache. She did little more than skim through them, then tied them again into a compact bundle.

Mildred thought back to the dark eyes smoldering with emotion, the slightly sullen obstinacy of the beautiful features, the impulsive manner in which Fern had acted. Mildred realized that the hitchhiker could have done almost anything on sudden impulse. She was the type to act in haste, to repent, if at all, at leisure. On hysterical impulse, the girl had sent the car plunging down the canyon. Then at the last moment had regretted her impulse to destroy herself and had tried to escape.

However, there was no use trying to recall the past. Mildred found herself face to face with reality. Didn't the death of Fern Driscoll, tragic as it had been, give her the longed-for chance of escape from all that lay behind her at Oceanside? Mildred sat there thinking for a long time before she finally went to bed.

So Mildred Crest became Fern Driscoll. She changed the color of her hair, and adopted dark glasses.

Mildred knew that with her secretarial ability she could land jobs without the slightest difficulty. It would, of course, be necessary to work out a story that would account for a lack of references. But Mildred felt certain that once she was given a test she would have little difficulty in finding work, references or no references.

The money in the purse bothered her. There was too much of it. She decided to hold this money as a sort of trust until she found out more about the girl whose identity she was borrowing.

The newspaper stories were exactly what Mildred had expected. The Oceanside paper carried quite a story. Mildred Crest, popular secretary of a local manufacturer, had been instantly killed in an automobile accident. In some way the driver had lost control, the car had gone over the grade on the Pala highway. The unfortunate girl had apparently been half-in and half-out of a right-hand automobile door when it struck against a huge rock near the bottom of the canyon. Afterward, the car had caught fire and the body had been partially burned before prompt action on the part of a passing motorist, who had a fire extinguisher in his car, had put out the blaze. The flames had started a brush fire which had not been extinguished until some two hours later.

Mildred studied the newspaper accounts and decided she was safe. Within twenty-four hours she had a job with the Consolidated Sales and Distribution Company under the name of Fern Driscoll, and within forty-eight hours felt herself well established.

Then almost immediately came the crushing blow.

Authorities were not "entirely satisfied." There had been a coroner's inquest. While much of the car had been consumed by fire, by a strange freak Mildred Crest's purse had not been consumed. The contents were quite recognizable. There were no bills in the purse, only change.

Authorities, moreover, found tracks indicating that someone had left the car after the wreck. Examination showed that the headlight and ignition switches had been turned off. Police felt it was quite possible that someone had crawled out of the window of the door on the driver's side of the car. There was to be a post-mortem examination of the burned body.

Mildred was in a panic. Would they discover the substitution of identities after that post-mortem?

Still going under the name of Fern Driscoll, because there was now nothing else for her to do, Mildred awaited the result of the autopsy.

She found it in a copy of the *San Diego Union*. The autopsy had shown that "Mildred Crest" had been dead *before* the fire started. There was some evidence of possible foul play. A service-station man had come forward who remembered putting gasoline in Mildred Crest's car. She had signed her name to the charge ticket. Then she had returned, canceled the charge, and paid cash. This caused the service-station attendant to remember the actual transaction.

The attendant at the service station remembered, moreover, that Mildred Crest had picked up a hitchhiker who presumably had been in the car with her at the time of the accident. It was suggested that this hitchhiker had perhaps killed Mildred in an attempted holdup. In the ensuing struggle the car had gone off the road.

The authorities had a good description of the hitchhiker, about twenty-three or twenty-four, five-feet-four, weight a hundred and twelve to a hundred and fifteen pounds, chestnut hair, brown eyes, well dressed, apparently from the Middle West.

Then came the last sentence of the story, the last paralyzing sentence. The autopsy had shown that the body of "Mildred Crest" had been in the second month of pregnancy.

Mildred dropped the paper from nerveless fingers. She understood everything now. Fern Driscoll, a young woman, probably of good family, in the second month of pregnancy—the disappearance, the forty, new hundred-dollar bills in the purse, the emergency fund to "see her through," the misery in the girl's eyes, the desire to keep going, yet having no fixed destination in mind.

And now that Mildred Crest had taken the identity of Fern Driscoll, now that she dared not disclose her true identity, she knew that Fern Driscoll's pregnancy had been transferred to Mildred Crest.

How the tongues would be buzzing in Oceanside!

The newspaper account had mentioned that the authorities were making a "determined effort" to find and question the hitchhiker who had presumably been in Mildred Crest's car at the time it went off the road.

As though it were not enough to be branded by the stigma of another girl's pregnancy, she was now suspected of her own murder.

Mildred Crest was very glad she had started wearing dark glasses the day after she arrived in Los Angeles. She wore them all the time. The bright California sun, she said, hurt her eyes after living all her life in the Middle West.

2

THE OFFICES of the Consolidated Sales and Distribution Company where Mildred worked happened to be in the same building and on the same floor as offices occupied by Perry Mason, the famous lawyer. Mildred had noticed Mason's name on the door to his offices, and she had often heard stories of the daring exploits of the famous lawyer and his ingenious defense of innocent persons accused of crime.

Once she had ridden up in the elevator with the attorney and, as she stood beside him, looking up at the keen, piercing eyes, the rugged, granite-hard features, she experienced a strange feeling of confidence.

Almost without realizing that she had done so, Mildred had made up her mind that, if the worst ever came to the worst, she would turn to Perry Mason for help.

Twice she actually had been on the point of going to Mason's office, asking his secretary, Della Street, to arrange an appointment.

Each time she desisted because of a subconscious fear that Mason might tell her that what she was doing was wrong, insist that she go to the authorities and make a clean breast of the situation.

The more Mildred thought that possibility over, the more such a course seemed absolutely suicidal. She had reached a decision and she resolved never to turn back. She couldn't and wouldn't retreat.

Mildred Crest had no close relatives. Her father had died before she was born, her mother when she was five.

She had been raised by an aunt who had died three years ago, so Mildred was on her own in every sense of the word.

Occasionally, there was a twinge of conscience as Mildred wondered about the background and connections of the dead girl whose name she had taken. But as day after day passed in a placid routine, she saw no reason for taking any radical step.

She practiced signing the name "Fern Driscoll," using the signature on the driving license as a pattern.

After repeated attempts, she was able to dash off a fairly good replica of Fern Driscoll's signature.

The forty one-hundred-dollar bills were still intact.

Mildred had secured a very satisfactory apartment. There was one long bus ride and then a short walk. The supermarket where she shopped was only two blocks away. Getting to and from the office and shopping represented Mildred's sole excursions into public life. She cooked her own meals in the apartment, kept to herself, formed no friendships at the office, but slowly and surely established her identity as Fern Driscoll.

Then one night out of a clear sky the blow fell.

It had been a hard day at the office. Mildred had worked overtime getting out some important letters. She had missed her regular bus. Dog-tired, she entered her apartment house. She had intended to stop by the supermarket, but she knew there were enough leftovers in the icebox to carry her through the evening, and there were eggs, bacon and toast for breakfast. She needed no more.

She hadn't even seen the man until she fitted her key to the door of the apartment. Then he materialized as from nowhere.

"Miss Driscoll?" he asked.

Something about the way in which he had been so inconspicuous as to defy notice and then the tense menace of his voice warned Mildred that this was no casual pickup.

She flashed him a quick look from behind her dark glasses.

"Well?" she asked.

The man nodded toward her key in the door of her apartment.

"Open the door," he said. "I'm coming in."

"Oh, no, you're not," she said, standing her ground. "Who are you? What do you want? How did you get in here?"

"The name wouldn't mean anything to you."

"Then you mean nothing to me."

"I think I do."

She shook her head angrily. "I'm not accustomed to being accosted by strangers in this manner. I'm going into my apartment and you're going to stay on the outside."

"I want to talk to you," he said, "about a certain automobile accident which took place near Pala; an accident where Mildred Crest met her death."

"I've never heard of Mildred Crest," she said. "I don't know about any accident."

He smiled condescendingly and said, "Listen, I don't want to make any trouble, but you and I have certain things to discuss and we'd better talk them over quietly."

"What is this, blackmail?"

His laugh showed genuine amusement. "Certainly not. I merely wanted to discuss the accident with you. I promise to be a gentleman, and if I'm not, you have the phone at your elbow. You can call the manager or the police—*if* you want the police."

"But I haven't the faintest idea what you're talking about."

"You will have, after you give me a chance to explain."

She remembered the woman who had the apartment across the hall, and Mildred had the uneasy feeling that she was listening. This woman was a thin, nervous busybody who had on several occasions tried to get acquainted, and the more reserved Mildred became, the more inordinate had been the other's curiosity.

She reached a swift decision.

"Very well. Come in," she said. "I'll listen to what you have to say and that's all. Then you're going out."

"Fair enough," the man said. "Just so you listen."

Mildred opened the door of the apartment.

Her visitor got down to brass tacks with a glib swiftness that indicated he had rehearsed the part he was to play.

"I'm Carl Harrod," he said, "an insurance investigator.

"We carried insurance on Mildred Crest's automobile. I was assigned to investigate the accident. The first thing I noticed was that Mildred had not been driving the automobile at the time it went over the bank. The next thing I noticed was that tracks indicated someone could well have walked away from the wreckage and gone down the canyon in the dark."

He paused and smiled apologetically. "I'm an investigator, I'm not a very good woodsman, and not a very good tracker, Miss Driscoll. But I did the best I could. I found tracks going down the canyon and finally I found what I was looking for; the place where you had climbed up out of the canyon.

"There was no money in Mildred's purse; that is, just a very small amount of change, yet I found she had gone to the bank and drawn out every cent she had on deposit, prior to the time she left Oceanside. There should have been more than five hundred dollars in the purse.

"For your information, Mildred Crest had received quite an emotional shock the day of her death. She had been keeping company with a young man who turned out to be an embezzler. He is now a fugitive from justice."

Carl Harrod settled back in the chair and smiled.

"Now then," he said, "it is quite apparent that Mildred Crest was dead before the fire was started. The trachea— the windpipe to you, Miss Driscoll—did not contain the faintest trace of the by-products of combustion. There were other things that the autopsy surgeon could tell, but I suppose you're not interested in the technical details. I think probably you know by this time that Mildred Crest was, unfortunately, in the second month of pregnancy.

"Putting these things together, it's possible to reach a very interesting and highly dramatic conclusion, a story which unfortunately is all too common."

Harrod smiled affably. "I'm not boring you, am I?"

"Go ahead," Mildred said.

"Our investigation was largely routine," Harrod said, "until I discovered the service station where Mildred had made her last purchase of gasoline. The attendant told me she had picked up a hitchhiker; that the hitchhiker had asked her where she was going and Mildred had said that she wasn't going anywhere.

"After I saw what had happened at the scene of the wreck, I naturally became interested in the hitchhiker. It really took only a slight effort to find you, Miss Driscoll. Your suitcase was in the car when it went off the road. The exterior was damaged by the fire, but I was able to trace the suitcase and finally to find the retailer who had sold it. His records disclosed your name.

"I felt perhaps you would come to the city and that you would look for work. It has taken me this long to locate you."

"What do you want?" Mildred asked.

"At the moment I want a signed statement from you," Harrod said.

"What sort of a statement?"

"I want a statement that you were driving the car at the time of the accident. I want a statement in your own handwriting as to just what happened and how it was that you left the automobile, stumbled down the canyon, finally climbed the bank and came here, all without reporting to the authorities anything that had happened.

"I would also like a signed statement from you that you took the money from Mildred's purse. This statement

22

would also release the insurance carrier from any liability, since you would admit that the accident was your fault.

"Now then, we come to a rather sordid part of the entire affair. Since you had an opportunity to take the money from Mildred's purse, since you had the opportunity to retrieve your own purse from the wreck, it is quite apparent that the fire didn't break out until an appreciable interval after the car had gone over the bank. It is, therefore, quite apparent that the fire was deliberately set in order to conceal the evidence of the theft.

"I would like a statement from you to that effect."

"Do you think I'm crazy?" Mildred asked.

Harrod shrugged his shoulders. "After all, these things are self-evident, Miss Driscoll. Why shouldn't you sign such a statement?"

"Don't be silly," she said. "I never knew Mildred Crest in my life. I wasn't in any automobile. I didn't—"

Her voice trailed away into silence.

Harrod's smile was patronizing. "Just stopped to think, didn't you, Miss Driscoll? You felt the fire would destroy a great deal of evidence. It destroyed very little, if any. A passing motorist who carried a fire extinguisher put out the fire in the car. Most of the gasoline had been spilled out of the tank when the car hit a rock at the top of the hill. That fire got out of control, but thanks to the fire extinguisher, the flames in the back of Mildred's car were extinguished.

"So I found the suitcase was sold to you in Lansing, Michigan. I made a little investigation at Lansing. You had charge accounts and an excellent credit rating. You left a good position in Lansing overnight without telling anyone where you were going."

"What do you intend to do with this statement if I should give it to you?" Mildred asked.

"Well," Harrod said, "that's an interesting question. Quite frankly, Miss Driscoll, I don't know myself. Theoretically I'm supposed to make a complete report on the situation and append the statement to the report. . . . Actually I don't think I'll do it."

"Why not?"

"I find you quite intelligent. You are very good-looking. Someday you will marry. You may even marry money. In short, I see unlimited possibilities."

"Blackmail!" Mildred said.

"Now, blackmail is a very crude and a very ugly word. Please remember, Miss Driscoll, that I haven't asked you for anything except a signed statement."

"I have no intention of writing any such statement."

"That, of course, *would* be your first reaction," Harrod said. "Well, you just got back from the office. I know that you're tired. You probably want to get your dinner and I see you would prefer to be alone.

"I'll let you think things over for a day or two, and then I'll be in touch with you again."

Harrod walked to the door, turned and smiled at Mildred. "I'll be back, Miss Driscoll," he said, "and please, *please* remember that I have asked you for nothing except a signed statement as to the facts. I am making that request in my capacity as an investigator for an insurance company. It is a thoroughly legitimate request, particularly in view of the fact that you might try to make a claim against my employer, Mildred Crest's insurance carrier.

"I mention this in case you should consult with some private detective agency, a lawyer, or even, in fact, the police. All I am asking for is a signed statement as to what happened. I would like to have you tell me this in your words.

"Anyone will tell you that is a customary procedure in cases of this sort.

"Thank you very much, Miss Driscoll. I've enjoyed our little visit. I'll see you again. Good night."

Harrod eased himself out of the door.

Mildred stood watching the closed door with sickening apprehension.

She had, indeed, burned her bridges.

What Harrod evidently didn't know as yet, but would probably find out, was about the forty hundred-dollar bills in Fern Driscoll's purse.

In view of her actions, it would now be impossible to explain how the fire had started. Harrod quite naturally assumed she had rifled the other girl's purse and had then started the fire to conceal the theft.

Either in the identity of Mildred Crest, who had stolen four thousand dollars from Fern Driscoll, or in the borrowed identity of Fern Driscoll, who had stolen some five hundred dollars from Mildred Crest, she was between two fires.

And, in the background, was the possibility of her being charged with first-degree murder.

3

DELLA STREET, Perry Mason's confidential secretary, said, "There is a young woman employed by the Consolidated Sales people down the hall who wants an appointment. She says it will only take a few moments and she'd like to run in and talk with you whenever it's convenient. She says she can get away for ten or fifteen minutes whenever we phone."

"Say what it's about?" Perry Mason asked.

"Only that it was a personal matter."

Mason looked at his watch, then at his appointment schedule, said, "These things that take only fifteen or twenty minutes quite frequently take an hour, and you don't like to throw a girl out right in the middle of her story. We have a half-hour, though. . . . Give her a ring, Della. Ask her if she can come in right away. What's her name?"

"Fern Driscoll."

"Do you know her?"

"I don't think so. She says she's seen me in the elevator. I think she's new with the company."

"Give her a buzz," Mason said, "tell her I can see her right away if she wants to come in now. Tell her that's with the understanding it will only take twenty minutes; that I have another appointment."

Della Street nodded and went to the telephone.

A few moments later she was back saying, "She's coming in right away. I'll go to the reception office and meet her."

"Skip the preliminaries," Mason said, "getting her name, address and all that. We'll get them when she comes in. I want to hear her story and rush things along as much as possible."

Della Street nodded, went to the reception office and within less than a minute was back. Turning to the young woman she had escorted into the office, Della Street said, "This is Mr. Mason, Miss Driscoll—Fern Driscoll, Mr. Mason."

"Sit down, Miss Driscoll," Mason said. "You're working for the Consolidated Sales and Distribution Company, I believe."

"Yes, sir."

"Where is your residence, Miss Driscoll?"

"309 Rexmore Apartments."

"What did you want to see me about?" Mason asked. And then added in a kindly manner, "I specialize mostly in trial work and a good deal of it is criminal work. I think perhaps you're in the wrong law office, but I may be able to help you get in touch with the right man."

She nodded briefly, said, "Thank you," then went on, "you'll have to pardon my dark glasses. Ever since I came to California some two weeks ago I've been having eye trouble—I hitchhiked and I feel as if the retina of my eyes became sunburned. Did you happen to read in the paper some two weeks ago about a Mildred Crest of Oceanside who was killed in an automobile accident?"

Mason smiled and shook his head. "These automobile accidents are a dime a dozen. They are usually all grouped together on an inside page. Was there something special about Mildred Crest's death?"

"I was riding with her when she was killed."

"I see," Mason said, eying her sharply. "Were you hurt?"

"Fortunately I was only bruised a little. I was sore for a day or two, but that was all."

Mason nodded.

"Mr. Mason," she said, "so that you can understand the situation, I have to tell you certain things.

"I lived in Lansing, Michigan. I wanted to disappear for reasons of my own. I can assure you I haven't violated any laws. I just wanted to get away where I could begin all over again. I was restless and nervous. I had sufficient funds to buy a ticket to any place I wanted to go, but the point was I didn't know where I wanted to go. I was drifting aimlessly. I was hitchhiking."

"Go on," Mason said.

"I went to Phoenix, stayed there for a few days, then went to San Diego, stayed there for only a few hours, got a ride out of San Diego and got as far as a little place called Vista and I was, for the moment, stranded there. It was about . . . oh, I don't know, seven-thirty or eight o'clock in the evening. It was dark and this Mildred Crest drove up."

"You knew her?" Mason asked.

"No, I was simply waiting there at the service station for a ride. You see, a young woman on the highway is a little different from a man. A man will stand out by a boulevard stop and try to thumb a ride. Anyone who stops is a good ride. But not many people stop.

"However, a young woman on the highway has plenty of rides. Almost every car stops and offers her a lift, but—Well, I don't care to play it that way. I like to be at a service station where I can size up the person and then ask if I may ride."

"So you asked Mildred Crest for a ride?"

"Yes."

"And what happened?"

"I sensed at the time that Mildred Crest was running away from something, that she was very much upset and— Well, for instance, I asked her where she was going and she said, 'Away.' "

"So what did you do?"

"Well, that was so exactly my own case, I asked her if I could go along with her, and she said, 'All right.' I don't know. I think we might have confided in each other after a while. I had troubles of my own and she certainly had plenty on *her* mind.

"However, we drove down to Pala and then turned on the road going up from Pala and there was an accident."

"What happened?"

"There was an accident. Another car met us right on a hairpin turn. I tried to avoid—I mean, it was impossible to avoid the other car entirely. It was going too fast. It just barely sideswiped us, just a little bit, but enough to put the car out of control and over the embankment. The car went down and Mildred, I guess, opened the door and tried to get out of the car before it went over, but she didn't have time. The door was unlatched and she was halfway out when the car went over. She struck her head against a rock and— Well, she died instantly."

Mason thought for a moment. "Who was driving the car?" he asked.

She took a deep breath. "At the time, I was."

"How did that happen?"

"Well, after we started out we talked a little bit and I could sense that Mildred was emotionally upset. She asked me if I drove and I said I did and she started to cry and tried to wipe the tears from her eyes while she was driving. So I offered to take the wheel and she said perhaps I'd better for a little while."

"Did you pick the roads or did she?"

"She told me where to go."

Mason said, "If you went from Vista to Pala and then turned at Pala and started back up the grade, you were just doubling back on yourself and—"

"I know. I think eventually she intended to return to Oceanside, but— Well, as it afterward turned out, there were reasons why—"

"Oh, I remember the case now," Della Street interjected. She turned to Perry Mason and said, "You may remember it, Chief. We commented briefly about it. The girl had just learned her fiancé was wanted for embezzlement. The autopsy showed she was pregnant."

"Oh, yes," Mason said, looking at his visitor with renewed interest. "She didn't tell you anything about this?"

"No. I think she would have, but, as I say, there wasn't time. We were just getting acquainted when the accident happened."

"All right," Mason said, "why did you come to me?"

"Because I . . . I was trying to disappear. I certainly didn't want my name in the paper and I was afraid that, if the newspapers published that Fern Driscoll of Lansing, Michigan, was in the car, there would be an exchange item, or however it is they work those things, and the Lansing paper would get hold of it and— Well, you know the way they do, publish a little paragraph under headlines: 'LOCAL GIRL INVOLVED IN CALIFORNIA TRAFFIC ACCIDENT.' I just didn't want that. I wanted to keep out of the whole thing."

"So what did you do?" Mason asked.

She hesitated a moment, said, "I— Well, I'm afraid I was negligent. I am responsible for the car catching fire."

"How did it happen?"

"I found that I wasn't hurt. I squirmed out through the window on the left-hand side of the car. The door wouldn't open but the window was down. I was pretty badly shaken up and I guess pretty rattled. I struck a match and took stock of the situation. I wanted to see if I could help the other girl."

"Mildred?"

"Mildred."

"And what happened?"

"As soon as I saw the way she was lying, half-in and half-out of the door and her head— I . . . I just became terribly nauseated. It was frightful. She had been half-out of the car and her head had been— Well, it was smashed! Just a pulp!"

Mason nodded.

"After that it took me a little while to get myself together and, of course, all of that time gasoline was running out of the car. Apparently it was leaking out of the tank at the rear of the car and trickling down toward the front. I didn't know just what was happening and I'm afraid I'm responsible for not appreciating the danger. Anyhow, I struck a second match and that second match burned my fingers, so I dropped it. There was a flash and I jumped back and the whole thing started blazing into flame."

"You didn't have your hair or eyebrows singed?" Mason asked.

"No, I was holding the match down and— Well, that's the way it was."

"So then what did you do?"

"I had my purse with me, fortunately. I— My suitcase, with everything I own, was in the car. I started running from the fire and then I found myself at the bottom of a little canyon. . . . And then I guess I got in something of a panic. There was a rattlesnake that I almost stepped on and— Well, by the time I got up to the road, I just wanted to get away from there without having my name in the papers or anything, so— Well, that's what I did."

"You didn't report the accident to anyone?"

She shook her head.

"How long ago was that?"

"About two weeks, not quite. It was the twenty-second."

Mason's eyes narrowed.

"And some development has caused you to come to see me?"

"Yes."

"What?"

"A man by the name of Carl Harrod called on me last night. He's an investigator for the insurance company. From the position of the car and the manner in which the doors were jammed, it was apparent that only the person who was in the driver's seat could have squirmed out through the window. My suitcase was in the car, it wasn't entirely consumed by the fire. The fire burned uphill and some of the things in the front of the car weren't even damaged. A motorist with a fire extinguisher saved the car. Mildred's purse wasn't burned up. . . . Well, anyway, this man Harrod had put two and two together. He found out that Mildred had picked up a hitchhiker at Vista and then he traced the hitchhiker back from Vista, which wasn't too difficult to do.

"You see, a woman hitchhiker who is—" She broke off to smile at Mason and said, "All right, I'll use the term good-looking, naturally attracts some attention. I had given my right name to one of the people who picked me up and then there was the clue of the suitcase and— Well, that's the way it was."

"And what did Harrod want?" Mason asked.

"He wanted me to sign a statement."

"In regard to the accident?"

"Yes."

"Did you do it?"

"No."

"Why?"

"Because I . . . I have the feeling Mr. Harrod wants that statement not on behalf of the insurance company but— I think he wants to do something with it."

"Blackmail?" Mason asked.

"I wouldn't be too surprised."

"Did he make any overtures along that line?"

"He intimated something like that. Later on, he was very careful to point out that he actually had asked for nothing except a written statement."

Mason drummed with the tips of his fingers on the top of his desk. His eyes were squinted thoughtfully.

"So," she asked, "what do I do?"

Mason said, "You've gone this long without reporting an accident. That is bad. But sit tight and wait for another twenty-four or forty-eight hours. If Mr. Harrod calls to see you again, I want you to tell him only what I shall tell you to tell him."

"What's that?"

"You have a pencil?"

She shook her head.

Mason nodded to Della Street.

Della Street handed the young woman a shorthand notebook and pencil.

"You take shorthand?" Mason asked.

"Oh yes."

"All right, take this down," Mason said. "Here is what you tell Mr. Harrod. Simply say, quote, Mr. Harrod, I have consulted my attorney, Mr. Mason, about all matters in connection with your previous visit. Mr. Mason has advised me that, if you call on me again, I am to ask you to get in touch with him. So, therefore, I ask you to call Mr. Perry Mason, who is representing me in the matter. If his office doesn't answer or if it is night, call the Drake Detective Agency and leave word with Mr. Paul Drake. Mr. Mason is my lawyer. Aside from that, I have nothing to say. I don't care to discuss the matter with you. I don't care either to confirm or deny any deductions you may have made. I am, in short, referring you to Mr. Mason for all information concerning the matter under discussion."

Mason watched the pencil fly over the page of the notebook with deft, sure strokes.

"You're evidently a pretty good stenographer," Mason said.

She smiled. "I think I am. I'm fast and accurate."

Mason glanced at his watch. "All right. That's all *you* do. Just tear that page out of the notebook, read it over enough so you remember it, and if Mr. Harrod calls, refer him to me."

She detected the note of dismissal in his voice, got to her feet. "How much do I—?"

Mason waved his hand. "Forget it," he said. "You're employed on the same floor here in the building, which makes you something of a neighbor, and after all there's nothing— Wait a minute, do you have a nickel in your purse?"

"Why, yes."

"All right," Mason said, smiling, "give me the nickel. That means that I've been duly retained to protect your interests and anything you have told me is a privileged communication. Also, anything I have told you is entirely confidential. Now then, go back to work and quit worrying about Mr. Harrod. If he becomes a nuisance, we'll find some way to deal with him."

Impulsively she gave Mason her hand. "Thank you so much, Mr. Mason."

Mason held her hand for a moment, looked at her searchingly, said, "All right, Miss Driscoll. . . . You're certain you've told me all of it?"

"Yes, yes. Of course."

"All right," Mason told her. "Run along back and get to work."

When she had left the office, Mason turned to Della Street.

"What do you think, Della?"

"She's really frightened. Why did you tell her not to report the accident? Didn't you take a risk doing that?"

"Probably," Mason said. "However, I didn't want her to get in any worse trouble than she is now. Her story of what happened isn't true. I don't want her to make a false report."

"In what way isn't it true?"

"The other car didn't crowd her off the road. Notice she said, 'It was impossible to avoid the other car entirely.'

"No one on earth ever described an automobile accident of that sort in that way. A person would have said, 'Although we got way over on our side of the road, the other car hit us.' "

Della Street thought that over, then nodded thoughtfully.

Mason said, "Now that you know this Fern Driscoll, you'll be seeing her in the elevator and in the rest room. Keep an eye on her and see if she doesn't try to find some opportunity to confide in you. I have an idea the situation will change within the next forty-eight hours."

"And I'm to report to you?" Della Street asked.

"That's the idea," Mason said.

4

■

THAT NIGHT after Mildred had cleaned away the dinner dishes, put the apartment in order, the chimes on the apartment door sounded.

She took a deep breath, set her face in the expression she wanted to use on Carl Harrod and opened the door.

The young woman who stood on the threshold was perhaps twenty-one or twenty-two. She had a dark complexion with finely chiseled features, a chin that was up in the air far enough to indicate pride, breeding and a certain strength of character.

Gray eyes made an appraising study of Mildred.

"Well?" Mildred asked at length, breaking the silence.

"Oh, Fern," the young woman said, "I— It *is* Fern Driscoll, isn't it?"

Mildred nodded.

"I'm Kitty Baylor," the young woman said, as though that explained everything. And then she added, by way of explanation, "Forrie's sister."

"Oh," Mildred said, striving to get her mind adjusted so she could cope with this new complication.

"I know," her visitor said, the words rushing out rapidly, "I'm the last person in the world you expected to see, the last person on earth you *wanted* to see. However, there are certain things we're going to have to face. Running away from them doesn't help.

"I'm up at Stanford, you know, and when I found out about what had happened— Oh, Fern, please let me come in and talk things over. Let's see if we can't find *some* sort of a solution."

Mildred stood to one side. "Come in," she invited.

"I'd heard about you from Forrie," Kitty Baylor went on. "I . . . I don't know how to begin."

Mildred closed the door. "Won't you sit down?" she invited.

Mildred's visitor seated herself, said, "We've never met but you undoubtedly know about me and I know about you."

Kitty Baylor paused, and Mildred nodded dubiously, sparring for time.

"Now then," Kitty went on, "if it's a fair question, would you tell me just *why* you suddenly packed up and went away, why you left all of your friends, your contacts and simply disappeared?"

Mildred said with dignity, "I don't think I have to account to you for my actions."

"All right," Kitty said, "I'll put my cards on the table. This is going to hurt. I don't like to say some of the things I'm going to have to say, but I guess I've got to."

Mildred said nothing.

Kitty took a deep breath. "I'm interested in protecting your good name just as much as the good name of my family. I . . . I guess there's only one way of saying what I have to say and that's to be brutally frank. You and Forrie were friendly. You were *very* friendly. I *know* that."

Kitty paused and Mildred said nothing.

Kitty fidgeted for a moment, then pushing up her chin and looking Mildred in the eyes said, "A man whom Dad regards as a blackmailer has been trying to build up the facts for a scandal story. This man is going to publish a story in a slander magazine that makes a specialty of digging out dirt with a sex angle.

"That story concerns you. Are you interested?"

Mildred tried to say something, but couldn't.

"All right," Kitty went on, "I'll tell you what that story is. It's that you and Forrie were living together, that you became pregnant, that Forrie went to Dad, that Dad was furious, that he felt Forrie had jeopardized the good name of the family, that you were given a large sum of money to go away and have your baby, that you wanted Forrie to marry you, but that Dad wouldn't let Forrie even consider it and that Forrie was under Dad's domination."

Kitty paused and Mildred, not knowing what to say, maintained an embarrassed silence.

Kitty seemed to shrink within her clothes. "Well," she said, "I guess it's true. I'd have sworn it wasn't. I wouldn't have thought Dad would have done a thing like that. I *know* he wouldn't. He admits that he talked with Forrie about you and said in a general way that he hoped Forrie would marry in his social set. I guess it's no secret that Dad wanted and I guess he still wants Forrie to marry Carla Addis."

Kitty, suddenly weary, said, "I know I'm taking an awful lot on myself, but this *is* important. It's important to all of us. Do you want to say anything?"

Mildred shook her head.

"All right," Kitty went on, "here are my cards all face up, Fern. If the story is true, I'm on your side. If you are pregnant and were sent away like that, I'm going to do something about it.

"You're a woman. I'm a woman. I think you care for Forrie. I'm his sister and I love him. I know he has faults. I know, too, that Dad thinks altogether too much about family and social position and perhaps he's talked Forrie into his way of thinking."

Mildred remained silent.

"On the other hand," Kitty went on, her eyes boring directly into Mildred's "it may just be what Dad thinks, some sort of blackmail scheme by which you're planning to hold up the family, blast Forrie's future with a paternity suit, or team up with this man Harrod for a shakedown. If so, you're headed for trouble, and I mean big trouble. Dad is a fighter, and you just don't have any idea how hard he can fight. You're buying yourself a ticket to the penitentiary for blackmail."

"I came here to find out the truth."

Mildred met Kitty Baylor's eyes, said suddenly, "I'm sorry. I can't tell you what you want to know."

"Why not?"

"Because," Mildred said, "I don't know."

Kitty's eyes were suspicious. "You mean you don't know whether you're going to have a baby?"

"It isn't that," Mildred said. "It's . . . it's—"

"Is it a shakedown? Are you in need of money?"

"It isn't that. It's—I don't want to—"

Mildred rose abruptly, crossed to the window and absently watched the traffic in the street below. Then she turned suddenly. "All right, I guess I'm going to have to tell you.

"Will you promise not to interrupt and let me tell you the whole story in my own way?"

"Of course. Go ahead."

Mildred waited for a couple of seconds, then plunged ahead.

"I'm not Fern Driscoll!"

Then slowly, in detail, Mildred told Kitty exactly what happened the night she had picked up Fern Driscoll and about the visit she had had from Carl Harrod.

"So there probably *is* something to the claim this man Harrod is making," Mildred finished up. "*He* thinks I'm Fern Driscoll. I don't think he even suspects any switch in identity."

Kitty Baylor blinked her eyes as she tried to adjust herself to this new situation.

At length she asked, "Are you—? I mean . . . are you—?"

"No," Mildred said.

Kitty was silent for a few seconds, then she said thoughtfully, "I don't believe Harrod *really* does think you're Fern Driscoll. I think he's trying to get you to sign a statement as Fern Driscoll so he'll have you in his power. Then he can make you say or do almost anything he wants. He's on the track of a big story, something that he can make into a really sensational scandal feature. I'm terribly sorry about Fern. I never knew her, but I know that Forrie was fond of her and— Good Lord, things really *are* in a sweet mess, aren't they?

"This worm, Harrod, really has a story. Sordid sex, surreptitious trysts between a secretary and the son of a wealthy manufacturer, then the arrogant father with the power of wealth. . . . You haven't fooled Harrod a bit. The more I think of it, the plainer it becomes. You see, Harrod told Dad that Fern was two months pregnant. He must have learned that from the autopsy."

"She could have told someone," Mildred said.

"I suppose so," Kitty said.

Mildred asked, "Why did she leave?"

"Probably because she was a darn decent kid," Kitty said. "She must have been in love with Forrie. She went away so she wouldn't bring any disgrace on Forrie. Even if they married, she knew that the child would come too soon and— No, Forrie wouldn't have let her go."

Mildred said, "No one knows this, Kitty, but there were four thousand dollars in Fern's purse, forty, new one-hundred-dollar bills."

Kitty looked at her with wide-eyed dismay. "Where's the money now?"

"I have it."

"Good Lord!" Kitty said. "That would make Harrod's story even better! The poor, little secretary finding herself pregnant tries to get the son of the wealthy manufacturer to marry her. The manufacturer kicks her out into the cold, cruel world giving her four thousand dollars to go and have her baby. Mildred, it *can't* be true!"

"Well, she had four thousand dollars in her purse," Mildred said flatly. "I don't know where she got it. And the autopsy showed she was two months pregnant."

Kitty put her hands to her temples. "What a mess! Did Harrod get anything out of you, Mildred?"

"I told him nothing," Mildred said. "I went to Perry Mason, the lawyer. If Harrod returns, I'm to tell him this." She read her shorthand notes.

Kitty Baylor's eyes showed sudden enthusiasm. "That's it! That's the solution. We'll let Perry Mason deal with that dirty blackmailer."

"The hitch there is, he won't go to Perry Mason," Mildred said. "If, as you suspect, he knows that I'm masquerading as Fern Driscoll, he's just going to set a trap and—" She broke off at the sound of the door chimes.

"That may be Harrod now," Mildred said as she arose and started for the door.

Kitty motioned her back. "Wait a minute," she whispered.

Mildred paused.

"Look, if it's all right with you I'll go to the door and tell him that *I'm* Fern Driscoll, ask him what he means by saying that I'm pregnant, and slap his face. Is that okay by you?"

"He doesn't know you by sight?" Mildred asked, in a low voice.

Kitty shook her head.

"It's all right with me," Mildred said, "only I don't think you'll get away with it. I think he knows it was Fern Driscoll who was killed in the accident. . . . And when you slap his face, he'll punch you in the jaw. A character like Harrod isn't governed by the conventions about not striking a woman."

"Leave it to me," Kitty said, and strode into the little hallway.

Mildred heard the sound of the latch being thrown

back on the door, then Kitty Baylor's voice saying, "I guess you don't know me. I'm—"

She was interrupted by Carl Harrod's voice. "Don't tell *me!* *I'll* tell *you!* You're Miss Katherine Baylor. Let me introduce myself. I'm Carl Harrod!"

Kitty Baylor's voice lost its assurance. "How—? How do you know who I am? I've never met you!"

Harrod's laugh was confident. "Just remember that I'm not an amateur at this game. Let's say that I've been casing the joint. I might even have followed you from the exclusive Vista del Camino Hotel, knowing that your family always stays there and feeling certain that some member of the family would be showing up to try and patch things up. . . ."

"All right, Mr. Harrod," Kitty interrupted. *"I've* been looking for *you.* Now let *me* tell *you* a few things!

"In the first place, if you desire any further communication with the occupant of this apartment, you are to contact Mr. Perry Mason, her lawyer. If it's after office hours, and if it is urgent, call the Drake Detective Agency.

"In the second place, Mr. Carl Harrod, having delivered that message, let me give you a simple, forceful, personal message, indicative of the respect in which I hold you."

There was the smacking sound of a hard slap, a profane exclamation in a masculine voice, and then the slamming of the door and the rasp of a turning key.

Kitty Baylor was back, her face flushed, her eyes shining.

"Harrod!" she spat. . . . "Where do I wash my hands?"

Mildred indicated the bathroom.

While Kitty Baylor washed her hands, Mildred reached her decision. "Look, Kitty," she said as Kitty emerged, "I would like to continue as Fern Driscoll. After all, if Fern Driscoll is dead, I don't see what difference it's going to make. Harrod may suspect that I'm not Fern, but as long as I'm using Fern Driscoll's name and her identity, he may be a little cautious. It's one thing to print accusations about a dead girl who can't defend herself, and quite another to make charges like that against someone else.

"If it's all right with you, I'd like to keep on being Fern Driscoll, because I don't want to go back to being Mildred Crest. It would be good from your point of view, too. When it appears that there isn't going to be any illegitimate child, the magazine won't dare to go ahead with Harrod's story. What about it?"

Kitty thought things over. "When you opened Fern's purse, you found four thousand dollars?"

"Yes."

"Tell me, was there anything else? Anything that would help us?"

Mildred shook her head.

There was a silence during which Mildred was thinking furiously. She had no right to turn the letters in Fern's purse over to Kitty. Yet what was she to do with them? She must keep herself in the clear. Technically, she knew she was obligated to turn all Fern's property over to the coroner, or some public official, or someone.

"All right," Kitty said suddenly. "If you want to keep on being Fern Driscoll, go right ahead, but I warn you there will be some difficult problems."

Mildred said wearily, "There are problems either way. ... I'm afraid of Harrod."

"He's a slimy blackmailer."

"I'm afraid of him just the same."

Kitty Baylor said abruptly, "I want you to promise me one thing, Mildred. If you should hear from any of the other members of the family, don't mention the fact that I've been here. I'm not supposed to know anything about this, but if either my father or my brother gave Fern Driscoll money and told her to go away and have her baby—well, I want to know about it, that's all! I . . . I've had differences of opinion with them before, but this is very, very serious!"

Mildred remained thoughtful. "I wish you hadn't slapped Harrod."

"That trash!" Kitty said. "I'm going to show you how to deal with him."

"How?"

"You wait right here," Kitty said. "I'll be back in about fifteen minutes. I'll show you how you can handle him."

She slipped on her coat, started for the door.

"How did you find me, anyway?" Mildred asked.

With her hand on the knob, Kitty suddenly paused. "Now, that's something I should tell you about," she said. "Fern Driscoll wrote a letter to one of the girls in the accounting department, a girl whom she knew quite well. She said that the bottom had dropped out of things as far as she was concerned, and that she was leaving, she didn't want anyone to know where she was, that she was going to hitchhike to Los Angeles, to get a job and begin all over again.

"That girl knew that Fern was in love with Forrie, that there had been some trouble. She thought it was just a lovers' spat and that Forrie might want to know where Fern was. In case he did, she wanted Forrie to be able to find her without too much trouble.

"So, this girl sent Fern's letter on to me, telling me not to say where I got the information but, in case Forrie confided in me, I could use my discretion and tell him where Fern was, if I thought that was the thing to do.

"Later on, Margaret—that's my younger sister— wrote me that the family was facing a possible scandal on account of Forrie's affair with Fern Driscoll, that Dad was terribly worried, and that a man named Harrod was trying to blackmail him.

"So I hired a detective agency and told them that Fern

Driscoll was a secretary, a very competent secretary, that she had recently arrived in Los Angeles, and asked them to find her.

"I guess it was an easy job. They charged me thirty-five dollars, and gave me this address. I suppose you signed Fern's name to a utility application or something, didn't you?"

"To the telephone," Mildred said.

Kitty laughed. "Well, I guess it was *that* simple. I could probably simply have called information and got your number."

"Where are your father and your brother now?" Mildred asked.

"In Lansing, as far as I know. . . . You wait here, Mildred. I'm going out and get an ice pick for you."

"An ice pick!" Mildred exclaimed.

Kitty nodded. "It's a woman's best friend, the best weapon she can have. A sorority sister of mine tipped me off. Some police officer was the one who gave *her* the information.

"The hatpin used to be woman's traditional weapon, and believe me, it was a good one. A man instinctively recoils from something long and needle-pointed. This sorority sister of mine was in a community where they were having trouble with an exhibitionist. The police officer suggested that women who had to be out on the streets at night carry ice picks. You can put a cork over the point and slip it in a purse. Believe me, if you're ever out alone on a dark street, an ice pick can be worth its weight in gold!"

"You can't get an ice pick this time of night, and even if you could, I wouldn't want it," Mildred said.

"Oh, but I can! There's an arcade novelty store down a couple of blocks that's open and— You just try an ice pick on your friend Harrod and I can assure you, you won't have any more trouble with *him*."

44

5

WITH KATHERINE BAYLOR GONE, Mildred found herself in a panic. She feared Carl Harrod. She also realized now that Harrod must have discovered her impersonation and was playing with her as a cat plays with a mouse.

Why? He wanted something, and the fact that Mildred wasn't quite sure what it was he wanted was disquieting.

When the door chimes sounded again, Mildred's fear started her heart pounding. She went to stand by the door.

"Who is it?" she called in a thin, frightened voice.

"Kitty!" came from the other side of the door. "Open up . . . Fern!"

Mildred opened the door.

Kitty Baylor said, "I bring you weapons, my dear, the complete armory! Here you are! Three serviceable ice picks!"

"Three!" Mildred echoed.

"Three!" Kitty said, and laughed. "That's my bargain-hunting mind, I guess. They were priced at thirty-eight cents apiece, three for a dollar. I'm going to put one of them in *my* purse and carry it with me just in case.

"Harrod isn't going to lay a hand on me, not without getting an ice pick where he doesn't want it.

"Oh, don't look so horrified, Mildred. You don't have to *use* the things! It's simply the idea. A man can't stand having something like that jabbed at him.

"Now look, Mildred. I'm going to run on. I'm not going

to say a thing to anybody about what you have told me. I want to find out for myself certain things. I want to find out if either Dad or Forrie did give Fern Driscoll four thousand dollars and tell her to get lost.

"Something happened, and I want to know what it was. I tighten up every time I start thinking of what happened to poor Fern. Even if she did kill herself, it was the result of hysteria and temporary insanity. All that was caused by what she'd had to go through.

"Don't tell anybody that I've been here, and I won't tell anybody. If anything happens, and you need me, I'll be at the Vista del Camino tonight. When Dad's in town, he has the presidential suite, but I'll be in a modest two-room suite. I haven't checked in yet, just stopped by to leave luggage. They all know me at the hotel. You won't have any trouble reaching me.

"Now are you going to be all right?"

"I guess so."

"I'm going to leave these two ice picks on this little table right here by the door. If Harrod should come back, don't be afraid of him. All blackmailers are cowards.

"All right, I'm on my way. Thanks for putting your cards on the table, and here's luck!"

Kitty Baylor thrust out her hand and gripped Mildred's with firm, strong fingers.

"You think I shouldn't have run away, don't you?" Mildred asked.

"I don't know," Kitty said after a moment's hesitation. "However, there's no use worrying about it. It's done now. And if you want to be Fern Driscoll, go ahead. But remember this: Dad may be looking for you, and Forrie may be looking for you. I certainly hope Forrie does come to try and help you and . . . and to stand by the girl he— Good-by, Mildred."

When Kitty had gone, Mildred felt a little guilty because she had not told Kitty about the letters. She had confided in Kitty as to her own secrets, but instinct had been to leave what little veil of privacy remained about the affairs of Fern Driscoll. More and more, Mildred was coming to sympathize with the girl who had wrenched the steering wheel from her hands and sent the automobile plunging down to destruction.

Kitty hadn't been gone more than five minutes when the telephone rang.

Feeling certain she would hear Carl Harrod's voice, Mildred picked up the receiver.

The voice which came over the telephone was richly resonant with authority.

"Miss Driscoll?"

Mildred hesitated a moment. "Yes?"

"I'm Harriman Baylor, Fern. Now, what the devil's this story about the family having given you money to go ahead and disappear for a while. I—"

"*You* should know," Mildred Crest said, suddenly filled with a desire to avenge Fern Driscoll's memory.

"Well, I don't know!" Baylor said impatiently. "And if my son has been putting his neck in that kind of noose, I want to find out about it. Now tell me, do you know a man by the name of Carl Harrod?"

She hesitated a moment, then said, "He was here earlier this evening."

"I understand that Harrod is going to sell a story about this whole affair to some scandal magazine," Baylor went on, "and he says that you have some letters Forrester wrote you that are definitely incriminating, that you've made arrangements to turn those letters over to him. Is that true?"

"No."

"Do you have such letters?"

There was something in the authoritative timbre of the voice that had Mildred on the defensive.

"I have the letters," she said. "I haven't told anyone about them, nor have I turned them over to anybody."

"All right," Baylor said, "I want to talk with you. It's been a job finding you. I don't know what you're trying to— Well, anyway, I want to come and talk with you. I'll be seeing you."

The phone clicked. He hadn't asked for permission to call. He had merely said he was coming. Mildred sensed the man did everything like that. He was accustomed to taking the right of way.

Mildred suddenly realized that she had unleashed forces that she couldn't control.

Did Harriman Baylor know Fern Driscoll by sight? Would he know as soon as he saw her that she was an impostor? Knowing that she was an impostor, what would he do? Would he expose her?

Did Kitty really not know that her father was in town?

And what to do with those letters?

Kitty Baylor was right. Harrod was going to get her to make a statement of the accident and the removal of money from the purse. She would sign this statement as Fern Driscoll. Once she had done that, she would be pretty much within his power. And Harrod was really after those letters that had been in Fern Driscoll's purse.

Mildred had no intention of giving Harrod those letters. Neither, on the other hand, did she intend to turn them over to Harriman Baylor, the father of the man who indirectly had been responsible for Fern Driscoll's death.

Suddenly Mildred Crest knew that she didn't want to face Harriman Baylor. She knew too much, and yet about some things she knew too little.

Mildred picked up the purse, dropped the little packet of letters in it, hastily switched out the lights in the apartment and hurried to the elevator.

Finding the elevator was in use on the way up, she didn't wait but turned to the stairs and went down to the street.

6

PERRY MASON AND DELLA STREET were finishing dinner when the waiter said deferentially, "Excuse me, Mr. Mason, but the Drake Detective Agency asked you to call before you went out."

Mason nodded. "Anything important?"

"They didn't say, sir, just asked you to be sure and call before you left the restaurant."

Mason signed the check, nodded to Della Street, said, "Better give them a ring, Della. Find out what it is."

Della Street arose from the table and went over to the telephone booths.

Mason settled back in his chair, lit a cigarette, and surveyed the various people in the place with keen, observant eyes.

Della returned.

"What is it?" Mason asked.

"Well," she said, "we have two matters which would seem to require your attention."

"What are they?"

She said, "Fern Driscoll wants you to get in touch with her immediately. She says it's terribly important you see her. She seemed to be very upset, Drake's operator said. And you remember the blackmailer she told about, Carl Harrod?"

Mason nodded.

"He called up and asked you to get in touch with him about a matter of considerable importance to one of your clients. He left a number and an address, the Dixiecrat Apartments."

"He called the Drake Detective Agency?" Mason asked.

"That's right."

"Then he must have got that number from Fern Driscoll."

Della Street nodded.

"Well," Mason said, "let's make a couple of calls and see what it's all about. You have the numbers, Della?"

She nodded.

"First, we'll get Fern Driscoll at the Rexmore Apartments," Mason said.

He left the table, moved over to the telephone booths with Della Street.

Della's nimble fingers dialed the number. A moment later she said into the telephone, "Hello, Miss Driscoll. This is Della Street, Perry Mason's secretary. Mr. Mason will talk with you. . . . He's right here, Miss Driscoll."

Mason entered the telephone booth, said, "Hello, Miss Driscoll. What seems to be the trouble?"

Her voice came pouring over the wire. "Mr. Mason, a whole lot of things have happened. There were some things I didn't tell you about. I guess I held out a bit and— Well, there have been a lot of complications."

"Won't they keep until morning?" Mason asked.

"No. No. I— You see, there was someone, some intruder in my apartment, trying to get some things. He knocked me off my feet and I lashed out at him with an ice pick."

"Good work," Mason said. "Did you score?"

"I must have. The ice pick was jerked out of my hands and . . . and I can't find it."

"Did you report all this to the police?" Mason asked sharply.

"No, and there are reasons I don't want to. I— You understand, I can't. . . ."

Mason said, "Look, Fern, for a young woman who has a desire to remain obscure, you certainly do the damnedest things. Now, lock your door and try to keep out of trouble until I get there. You'd better tell me about this personally."

Mason hung up and said to Della, "Get this other number, Della. I'm afraid we're getting a lot of night work out of a five-cent fee."

"Aren't we," she laughed.

She called the number, said, "This is Miss Street, Mr. Mason's secretary. Mr. Perry Mason received a call from a Mr. Harrod. . . . Oh yes. Well, just a minute, I'll put Mr. Mason on."

Della Street said, "Some feminine voice. . . . Sounds attractive. . . . She said she'll call Mr. Harrod."

Mason picked up the phone, said, "Hello."

A man's voice started to say hello, then was checked in a fit of coughing.

"Hello, hello," Mason said impatiently. "I am calling Carl Harrod."

The voice said, "This is Harrod. . . . I wanted to talk with you. . . ." Again there was a fit of coughing.

Mason, frowning impatiently, said, "Hello. Just what was it you wanted?"

Harrod's voice, sounding weak, said, "Your client stabbed me in the chest with an ice pick. We'd better talk it over right away."

"Where did this happen?"

"At Fern Driscoll's apartment."

"Did you report this to the police?"

"Of course not."

"Why?"

"That isn't the way to handle something of this sort."

"What is the way to handle it?"

"Come over here and I'll tell you."

"Shouldn't you have treatment?"

51

"It isn't that serious, medically. It's damned serious legally."

"Stay there," Mason told him. "I think it's about time we had a talk."

"You *bet* it is!"

"Where are you?" Mason asked.

"I'm in my apartment at the Dixiecrat Apartments. Apartment 218."

"All right," Mason said, "that's not far from where I'm talking. You wait there. I'm coming over."

Mason hung up the telephone and said, "Now, this is a real run-around. Fern Driscoll found someone in her apartment and stabbed him with an ice pick. Apparently, she doesn't know where she hit him, but it was a solid enough blow so he took the ice pick away with him. Carl Harrod says she stabbed him in the chest.

"Hang it, Della, I suppose we've got to go take a look-see. Let's run up and have a quick talk with Fern Driscoll first, and get the thing straightened out. Then we'll try to put this blackmailer, Harrod, in his place."

"But shouldn't Fern Driscoll notify the police if—?"

"That's the devil of it!" Mason said. "She's keeping under cover and— The Rexmore Apartments is only five minutes from here by cab."

They left the restaurant, found a taxicab and went at once to the Rexmore Apartments.

Mildred Crest was anxiously awaiting them. She unlocked her door, seemed almost hysterically relieved as she held onto Mason's hand.

"All right," Mason said, "let's find out *exactly* what happened."

Mildred, on the verge of panic, said, "I'm going to have to give you a little personal history."

"Go ahead," Mason said.

"I left Lansing, Michigan, because— Well, there was a man by the name of Baylor, Forrester Baylor. His family didn't approve of me and— Well, it's a long story."

"Shorten it, then," Mason said crisply. "Let's have it."

"He had a sister, Katherine, a wonderful girl. I had never met her. She came here tonight and met me for the first time. She told me she sympathized with me and she thought the family had been perfectly horrid in the way they had treated me."

"What about the ice pick?" Mason asked.

"She bought them for me."

"Who did?"

"Kitty—Katherine Baylor."

"Bought *them*? Was there more than one?"

"Yes."

"Why?"

"She said blackmailers were yellow and that if I pointed an ice pick at Harrod and threatened him, he'd leave me alone."

"And at the same time make you guilty of assault with a deadly weapon," Mason said drily. "How many ice picks did she buy?"

"Three."

"Where are they now?"

"One of them is on the little table by the door."

Mason moved over to the table.

"There's only one ice pick here."

She nodded.

Mason lifted the ice pick.

"There's a price tag on here underneath transparent Scotch tape," he said. "The price tag says thirty-eight cents, three for a dollar. There's some fine print—let me see—oh yes, the imprint of the Arcade Novelty."

"The Arcade Novelty," Mildred explained, "is down the street a short distance. It's an arcade with a lot of penny machines for amusement. They cater largely to sailors and people who are lonely and want cheap entertainment.

"They have everything from electric machine guns for shooting at images of airplanes to girl shows on film machines. They call it a penny arcade, but most of the shows are a nickel or a dime."

"And they sell ice picks?" Mason asked.

"Not there, but in connection with it. There's a novelty shop where they have bottle openers, bottled goods, novelties of all sorts, a machine that vends ice cubes and things of that sort."

Mason nodded. "Now, tell me exactly what happened."

"I came in from the street. I snapped on the light switch, and the lights didn't turn on. Everything was dark."

"Could you see anything?"

"Just here by the doorway. The light came in from the main hallway so I could see a little. Someone was in here, searching the apartment."

"What happened?"

"I snapped the light switch two or three times. The light wouldn't come on. Then I heard someone move."

"Did you scream?"

"There wasn't time. I just had that feeling of motion coming at me, and instinctively I grabbed up one of those ice picks just as someone hit me."

"With his fist?"

"No, no! I don't mean it that way. Someone hit me like a football player hits a line. It was just a rush. I was bowled over."

"And what happened?"

"Well, I had the ice pick pointed out toward whoever was coming at me, and . . . and . . ." She began to sob.

"Now, take it easy," Mason said, "Let's get this thing straight."

She said, "The ice pick stuck into this person and he or she ran on past me and that jerked the ice pick out of my hands."

"The pick didn't fall to the floor?"

"No. Whoever was in here—well, the ice pick was carried away with him."

Mason thought things over for a moment, said to Della Street, "Della, go down to the Arcade Novelty. Get three of these ice picks, make it as fast as you can. Then come back here. The cab is waiting downstairs. Take it."

Mason turned to Mildred Crest. "Your friend Harrod called up. He said he'd been stabbed in the chest with an ice pick."

Mildred raised her clenched knuckles to crush them tightly against her lips. Her eyes were wide with terror.

Mason said, "You must have something in this apartment, something someone wants. You're hiding something. What is it? Money? Letters?"

"I . . . I'm supposed to have some letters. I think Harrod wants them very badly."

"What do you mean, you're *supposed* to have them!" Mason said.

"Well, you see— The letters were addressed to Fern . . . to me."

Mason watched her narrowly. "You say you're *supposed* to have them. Do you have them or don't you?"

"I . . . I have them."

"Where are they?"

"In my purse. I had them with me."

"Then why did Harrod want them?"

"To sell to a magazine, I believe."

Mason said, "Look here, young lady, you're lying to me. Are you really Fern Driscoll?"

There was panic in her eyes.

"Are you?"

"I . . . I can't talk now. I can't, I can't, I can't!"

She dropped into a chair, started sobbing hysterically.

Mason said, "Cut it out! Listen, there's no time for all that stuff. I don't know what we're getting into. If anything should happen and the police should question you, say that you refuse to make any statement save in the presence of your attorney. Can you do that?"

"Yes."

"*Will* you do it?"

"If you say so."

"I say so. Now, where's that missing ice pick? There were three. One's in Carl Harrod. Where's the other?"

"Kitty has it."

"What's her name?"

"Katherine Baylor."

"Where does she live?"

"She's at the Vista del Camino Hotel. She's from Lansing. Her family's rolling in money. Her father's Harriman Baylor, a big manufacturer. Her brother's Forrester Baylor. He's responsible for my condition—my pregnancy."

"How long have you been pregnant?"

"Two months. . . . No, no, Mr. Mason. I'm not really pregnant."

Again she started sobbing.

Mason looked at her with exasperation, then moved around the apartment looking at the drawers which had been pulled out and the contents dumped on the floor.

"We'll have to report this," he said.

"No, no! We can't! There are reasons. There isn't time to tell you everything now. I . . . I can't! I can't!"

Mason again turned away, looking around the apartment. He saw her purse on the chair, picked it up, opened it. "Are these the letters?"

She looked at the tightly tied packet. "Yes."

Mason put the letters in his pocket, looked again in the purse. Suddenly he said, "Where did you get all this money?"

She looked at him with tear-streaked eyes. "They're going to say I stole it—if they find it."

"Whose is it?"

"Fern Driscoll's."

56

"And you're not Fern Driscoll. You're Mildred Crest. Is that right?"

"Yes."

There was a knock at the door. Mason opened the door and Della said, "Well, here they are. Three ice picks, exactly the same as those others, but there's a different price tag on them."

"What do you mean?" Mason asked.

"They're forty-one cents straight now," she said, "but they were thirty-eight cents or three for a dollar."

"How come the price changed?"

"It's quite a story. The woman who rang up the sale dropped one, and when I picked it up I noticed the price for the first time. I inquired if the picks weren't three for a dollar. That's when she went into her long song and dance. It seems someone bought three picks earlier in the evening and this woman in charge went to replenish the stock in the display case and found there were only six left in stock. She says she orders them a gross at a time, so she made out an order for another gross and then found the price had gone up sharply since they had made their last order. So she tore the price tags off the others that were in stock and put the new price tags on them."

Mason turned to Mildred Crest. "Now look, Mildred, there isn't time to find out what this is all about now. I'm going to see Carl Harrod and find out about that ice-pick stabbing.

"Now, here are definite, positive instructions. If anybody comes and asks you about what happened, or about an intruder, or about stabbing anyone with an ice pick, you simply state that you have no comments to make. I am going to leave two of these ice picks here with you on the table. That will make a total of three.

"I want you to take all the price tags off all of these ice picks, flush them down the toilet and destroy them. You will then have three identical ice picks. If the police start checking and find that one woman bought three ice picks,

57

they'll find all three ice picks in your apartment. There won't be any missing."

"But won't they find out that—"

"Probably," Mason said, "if they start an investigation, but this will keep them from starting one unless they get a direct complaint. I'm taking these letters with me."

"Take the money, too."

Mason shook his head. "Keep that money right where it is. Put it in an envelope and mark it 'Property of Fern Driscoll.' Don't tell anyone anything about it. Don't answer questions about anything.

"Come on, Della."

Mason and Della Street left the apartment.

On the way down in the elevator, Della Street said, "What do I do with this extra ice pick?"

Mason said, "Harrod says my client stabbed him in the chest with an ice pick. Probably all he saw was a feminine figure silhouetted against light which was coming in from the corridor. He charged, doubtless intending to knock the woman over with the force of his charge and, while she was bowled over, make good his escape.

"That ice pick was invisible to him. It probably went in without any sensation of pain because the point was so fine and sharp. Later on, when he got out of the apartment house, he found an ice pick stuck in his chest. Harrod probably doesn't want to go to the police any more than our client wants to go to the police. So Harrod rang me up."

"And what does he want?" Della Street asked.

"That," Mason said, "is something we'll find out from Mr. Harrod himself. I have an idea that he wants to make a trade. I think he'll offer to trade his silence in return for some letters our client has.

"So," Mason went on, "the minute we get to Harrod's apartment, I'll do something to hold the attention of Harrod or whoever else is in the apartment. You plant this ice pick. Wear gloves, and be sure you don't leave any fingerprints."

"What about the price tag?"

"Leave it on."

"Why?" she asked. "If he was stabbed with an ice pick—"

"Exactly," Mason said. "I want it so *we* can tell the ice picks apart. The one that *you* planted and the one that someone stuck in his chest.

"If Harrod doesn't go to the police, we have simply presented him with an ice pick. If he does go to the police, the police will find two ice picks in his apartment. It will be up to Harrod to keep them straight so as to tell one from the other."

"Do I keep my gloves on all the time?" she asked.

"No," Mason said. "I have to explain your presence as my secretary. You plant the ice pick while I'm distracting their attention. As soon as you have the ice pick planted, take your gloves off and take out a notebook and pencil."

The cabdriver held the door open for them.

"Where to?" he asked.

Mason glanced significantly at Della Street.

"Drive straight down the street for three blocks," he said. "Then turn to the right and I'll tell you where we want to get out. We're meeting a person on a corner."

"Okay," the driver said. "I take it you want me to drive slow."

"That's right," Mason said.

The driver closed the door and the cab moved off, went down to the designated corner, turned to the right and moved slowly along.

They passed the Dixiecrat Apartments, went for half a block, then Mason said suddenly, "This is where we're to meet the person. Stop right here."

The driver stopped and Mason handed him a five-dollar bill. "This will cover the meter and leave you a little over," he said.

As the man started to thank him, Mason handed him two more one-dollar bills. "And this will enable you to buy something for the kids when you go home."

"Gee, mister, thanks," the cabdriver said. "I sure won't forget this."

Mason said, "In that case, perhaps you'd better give me the two dollars back."

The cabdriver thought for a moment, then grinned. "I've got the poorest memory in the world," he said.

Mason handed him three more one-dollar bills. "In a cabdriver," he announced, "that's a wonderful asset."

He and Della got out on the corner. The cab drove away. Mason and Della walked the half block back to the Dixiecrat Apartments.

Mason consulted the directory. "Carl Harrod, 218," he said.

Mason pressed the button.

Almost instantly the buzzer sounded which released the outer door.

"We could probably have saved time on the stairs," Della Street said, as the elevator slowly and reluctantly slid to a stop.

Mason opened the outer door, pulled back the sliding metal grill. Della Street entered, Mason followed her and pressed the button for the second floor.

As the elevator came to a dispirited stop, Mason pulled back the sliding metallic grill, opened the hinged door, let Della precede him into the corridor, and stood for a moment looking which way to turn.

A woman stood in the corridor six doors to the right.

Mason strode past Della Street to take the lead.

"Mr. Harrod?" Mason asked the young woman as he approached.

"You're Mr. Mason?"

"Yes."

"This way," she said. "Carl is expecting you."

She held the apartment door open and Mason walked in, preceding Della Street.

The woman waited until Della Street had entered the apartment, then hurried forward and said to Mason, "He's had a chill."

She led the way over to an adjustable reclining chair in which a man was stretched, a blanket wrapped tightly around him.

The eyes were closed.

"Carl," she said, "this is Mr. Mason."

Harrod opened his eyes. "I'm glad you came, Mr. Mason."

"You're Harrod?" Mason asked.

"Yes."

Mason bent over him and the young woman half-turned toward Della Street to invite her to be seated.

Mason said, "Is this Mrs. Harrod?"

The woman whirled to face him. There was a moment's embarrassed silence.

Then the young woman said, "Answer him, Carl."

Harrod waited a moment, said, "Yes, this is Mrs. Harrod."

Mason held the young woman's eyes. "How long," he asked, "have you been married?"

"And what difference does that make?" she blazed.

"I wanted to know," Mason said. "I'm an attorney. I'm dealing with an injured man. I want to know how long you've been married."

"It's none of your business!"

Mason noticed out the corner of his eyes that Della Street was moving swiftly around the apartment, as though looking for a comfortable chair. Abruptly she gave an exclamation of annoyance. "That pesky fountain pen! The cap is full of ink. I'll go to the sink and—"

Della darted through the door to a kitchenette. No one paid any attention to her.

Harrod said, "Look, honey, this is Mr. Mason. He's a lawyer. I think he's going to help us."

"I don't care what *you* think!" the woman said. "My private affairs are my private affairs and I'm certainly not going to have some smart lawyer come in and start putting *me* on the pan."

"No offense," Mason said. "I just wanted to know what the situation was."

"Well, now you know," she said.

"I'm not certain I do," Mason told her.

Della Street returned to the room, removed her gloves and took a notebook from her purse. "Where do you want me, Chief?" she asked.

Mason said, "This is Miss Della Street, my secretary. I want her to make notes of this conversation. Now then, you're Carl Harrod?"

The man nodded and coughed.

"You say you've been stabbed with an ice pick?"

"Yes."

"Where's the ice pick?"

"We have it," the young woman announced.

"I'd like to see it."

"We're keeping it where it's safe," she said.

"And just why do you think I'd be interested in this stabbing?" Mason asked.

Harrod opened his eyes, shifted his position slightly, moved his hands under the blanket, then lay still again. "You're going to be very much interested," he announced.

"Why?"

"You're representing Fern Driscoll."

"Did she stab you?"

Harrod was silent for a long moment. He closed his eyes, opened them, then said, "Who do *you* think?"

Mason said sharply, "I'm not here to play guessing games. I came here because you said a client of mine had stabbed you. Now, if you have anything to tell me, start talking. If you haven't, I'm leaving."

Harrod said, "Fern Driscoll stabbed me. She's your client."

"How did it happen?" Mason asked.

"I wanted to have a talk with her. I was investigating an automobile accident in which she was involved. I went up to her apartment."

"Where?" Mason asked.

"Rexmore Apartments. 309."

"Go on."

"I found the door slightly ajar. I pushed the button. I could hear the bell chimes on the inside. Abruptly the door was flung open and Fern Driscoll said, 'Oh, it's you!' and with that she lashed out at me—I didn't see the ice pick at the moment. I felt a sharp, stinging sensation at the skin. I didn't feel deep pain at all."

"Then what happened?" Mason asked.

"She slammed the door in my face, and locked it. There was someone else in there with her. I could hear them talking."

"What did you do?"

"I rang the chimes again, rattled the doorknob. I saw she wasn't going to open up, so I made up my mind I'd make her regret it. Believe me, I have the goods on her. I decided to release everything I had on her, and that's a lot."

"Go on," Mason said.

"Well, I turned for the stairs and that was when I found there was an ice pick in my chest."

Harrod turned to the young woman, said, "Nellie, how about a drink?"

She went through the door into the kitchenette, came back with a bottle of whisky and a glass half-filled with water.

"Only about half that water," Harrod said.

She dutifully went back to the kitchen, returned with the tumbler about a quarter full.

She extended the bottle and the glass, but Harrod said, "Pour it and hold it to my lips."

Harrod drank the whisky and water. The woman wiped his lips.

Harrod said, "It's funny but I've been cold ever since I got home."

"Have you had a doctor?" Mason asked.

"No."

"You'd better get one."

"I don't want one."

"Why?"

"Doctors ask too many questions."

"Did this ice pick go all the way in?" Mason asked.

"Clean to the hilt," Harrod said.

"Then you'd better have a doctor."

"I told you I don't want a doctor. Doctors go asking questions, and then they babble everything they know to the police."

"Well," Mason said, "it sounds to me as though the police should be notified."

Harrod shifted his eyes, said, "That would be bad for your client."

"I'll look out for the interests of my client," Mason said sharply.

"All right," Harrod said, "it wouldn't be good for me."

"Why not?"

"I am not the most exemplary citizen in the world, Mason," Harrod said. "I'm a— All right, I'm an opportunist."

"And a blackmailer?" Mason asked.

"He didn't say that," Nellie flared at Mason.

"I was trying to make it easier for him," Mason said.

"You don't have to!" Nellie snapped. "He can talk for himself."

Harrod said, "Fern Driscoll has some letters. I don't

know how much you know about her history, but she was going with Forrester Baylor in Lansing, Michigan. Forrester is the only son of Harriman Baylor, a big manufacturer.

"Fern Driscoll was working as his secretary. She and Forrester got playing around and then all of a sudden all hell broke loose. I *think* perhaps someone found out Harriman Baylor was about to become a grandfather under circumstances that didn't appeal to the old bastard."

"Watch your language," Nellie said sharply.

Carl Harrod grinned, went on talking, "I started out trying to sharpshoot. I'm an investigator for an insurance company. That's the way I make my bread and butter. I'm also an undercover correspondent for a magazine entitled *The Real Low-down.*

"I wasn't sure about my story until after I'd interviewed Fern Driscoll. Then I was certain I was on the right track. The trouble was the story is too big. The magazine has to have proof. I understand there are some letters written by Forrester. It's also reported that Harriman Baylor gave her a big wad of dough to go bye-bye and have a baby very quietly, then release it for adoption to anyone that Harriman Baylor designated.

"That's the kind of a story that *The Real Low-down* would pay ten thousand smackeroos to get nailed down.

"I have everything I need except the letters," Harrod said. "That's why I went to Fern Driscoll's apartment."

"You're telling me all this?" Mason asked.

"I'm telling you all this," Harrod said.

"And that secretary of his is writing every word of it down," Nellie snapped.

"Let her," Harrod said. "Mason has got to play ball with me in this thing."

"Go on," Mason said,

"I'd been there earlier and tried to be nice," Harrod

said. "Being nice didn't get me anywhere so I went back to try it again. This time I wasn't going to be so nice."

"Now, wait a minute," Mason said. "You went there the first time. What happened?"

"The door was opened by Katherine Baylor. I'd followed her to the place. You see, the Baylor family are out here quite often. Harriman Baylor has business interests in southern California. The family always stays at the Vista del Camino Hotel. I had a tip that Baylor himself had taken a tumble and was going to make a big try to get those letters.

"I felt certain some member of the family would show up. I had an idea they'd located Fern Driscoll. Katherine showed up, registered, left her baggage, and went right out to a cab.

"I followed in my car. She went direct to Fern Driscoll's apartment in the Rexmore.

"So I went up and rang the bell after she'd been there long enough to get the preliminaries over with."

"That was the first time you'd been to Miss Driscoll's apartment?" Mason asked.

"Actually it was the second time. . . . Suppose you let me tell it in my own way."

"All right," Mason said. "Go ahead."

"Well, Katherine came to the door, took a good look at me and after I'd introduced myself she used some strong language, then swung on me and cracked me on the nose."

"Then what happened?" Mason asked.

"I got a bloody nose. She slammed and locked the door before I could do a damned thing. I suppose she's accustomed to playing with people who are too gentlemanly to strike a woman. Believe me, if she hadn't got that door slammed and locked just when she did, I'd have broken her god-damned jaw."

"Your language, Carl!" Nellie admonished.

"Her god-damned jaw!" Harrod repeated, more emphatically and in a louder voice.

Nellie made clicking noises with her tongue against the roof of her mouth, indicating shocked disapproval.

"Go on," Mason said.

"All right. I went back after a while," Harrod said, "and knocked again. Believe me, if the door had opened and this Baylor bitch had been there, I'd—"

"Your language, Carl," Nellie said. "Mr. Mason's a lawyer."

"I mean, this Baylor girl," Harrod amended hastily, "if she'd been there, I'd have given her something to remember me by. That is, if she'd opened the door."

"She wasn't there?"

"I think she was," Harrod said. *"Someone* was in there with her. I could hear them talking. I don't know who it was."

"All right. What happened?"

"I've told you what happened. I rang the chimes. Fern Driscoll pushed open the door and lurched at me with this ice pick without so much as a word!"

"Not a single word?"

"Well, she said something like 'You again!' or something like that."

"Were the lights on in the apartment?" Mason asked.

"What do you mean, were the lights on?" Harrod countered.

"When the apartment door was opened," Mason said, "were lights on in the little reception hallway of the apartment?"

Harrod thought for a moment. "I don't remember. Why?"

"I was wondering why you didn't see the ice pick so you could avoid it," Mason explained. "You wouldn't have just stood there while someone made a pass at you with a weapon like that."

Again Harrod thought for a moment, then said, "I

guess you're right. I sure as hell didn't see any ice pick. The lights weren't on in the apartment. That is, they may have been on in the apartment itself, but the door opens into a little hallway. When you go in the door, there's a little, narrow hallway, then you make a sharp, right-angle turn to the left and then you come into the main apartment."

"And you had no idea you had been stabbed with an ice pick until *after* the door closed?"

"That's right."

"And you didn't *see* the ice pick?"

"No."

"Then you couldn't have seen the face of the woman who wielded the ice pick clearly enough to be absolutely certain," Mason said. "As far as *you* know, it could have been Katherine Baylor who stabbed you instead of Fern Driscoll."

Harrod's face showed anger. "You've got no right to come up here and cross-examine me and— Damn it, I'm trying to be co-operative. Now I'll make you a proposition, Mason."

"What is it?"

"Your client can make a settlement with me. Your secretary there can type up a release and I'll sign it."

"What sort of a settlement?"

Harrod shook his head. "You go talk with your client, then *you* make *me* an offer. You've heard my story, now go get hers. Get it all. Don't take anything for granted. Ask her who she *really* is. *Then* you come back to me."

Mason said, "Not now, Harrod. First we're going to have a doctor look you over and see how serious the situation is."

"I don't want a doctor. I know exactly what I want."

Mason said, "I'm going to get my own personal physician on the job. He's going to give you a once-over. The idea is to keep any complications from developing."

"I told you I didn't want a doctor. He'll ask me questions and then go to the police. Once he does that, we're all in the soup."

"That," Mason interrupted, "is the beauty of having *my* doctor on the job instead of yours. He'll ask you how you feel, he'll take your blood pressure, he'll find your exact physical condition. He may ask you questions about how it happened, and, if he does, you're perfectly free to tell him that, for all you know, you were walking in your sleep, stumbled, and fell forward on an ice pick. Or you can simply refuse to answer questions, and tell him that you'll talk to your own doctor at the proper time."

"But what good is it going to do to have this doctor of yours see me?"

"It may save some complications," Mason said. "He'll be my doctor. Not yours. He'll be appraising the injury so as to assess damages."

"I don't need to tell him how it happened?"

"No."

"It won't cost me anything?"

"Nothing."

There was a moment's silence.

Mason went on, "There are some disadvantages. The doctor won't report to you. He'll report to me. But if he feels you should have any special treatment, he'll tell me. That will be to your protection.

"Because he's my doctor instead of yours, you won't have to answer any questions that you don't want to answer, and if he doesn't have any information from you that indicates you were the victim of a felonious stabbing, he won't have to make a report to the police."

Harrod grinned. "Particularly if I tell him that I was holding the ice pick in my hand when my wife pushed open the door carrying a bunch of dishes in from the kitchen, and that the door hit my hand and rammed the ice pick into my chest."

"Don't let him trap you," Nellie warned. "That's exact-

69

ly what he wants you to do; make some contradictory story to a doctor and—"

Harrod's face showed anger. "Shut up!" he said. "Keep your big bazzoo out of this!"

"Watch your language!" she said.

Harrod laughed. "Your bazzoo, I said, sweetheart. Your *bazzoo!*"

He turned to Mason, said wearily. "That's what comes of teaming up with an illiterate broad who tries to be refined."

Nellie sucked in a quick breath, started to say something, then changed her mind.

"How long will it take you to get your doctor here?"

"He should be here within an hour."

"What's his name?"

"The one I have in mind is Dr. Arlington."

"He's worked for you before?"

"Yes."

Harrod said to Nellie, "Give me another blanket, Nellie. I'm still cold." He turned to Mason, said, "Here's something you can be thinking about in the meantime. Your client can't stand an investigation. Don't let her pull the wool over your eyes. She isn't Fern Driscoll. She's Mildred Crest. She stole Fern Driscoll's purse, her identity and her money.

"You just let that broad of yours know that you know that, and that I know it. Then you come back and we'll talk a little turkey.

"Now then, go get your doctor if that will make you feel any better."

70

7

MASON AND DELLA STREET called Dr. Arlington, then took a taxicab to the place where Mason's car was parked and drove back to the Dixiecrat Apartments.

They had waited some five minutes when Dr. Arlington drove up, parked his car ahead of Mason's, got out, shook hands, and said, "What's it all about, Perry?"

Mason said, "It's a damage claim. That is, it's going to be a damage claim. The man's name is Harrod. He's in Apartment 218. I told him I was sending my doctor. You ring the bell, go on up and take a look at him. Be sure you have it definitely understood that you are there as my physician, making an independent checkup. Explain to him that you are not his doctor, and that there is to be no confidential relationship of physician and patient. If he makes any statement to you about how he feels, I want you to be able to testify."

"All right," Dr. Arlington said. "What seems to be the trouble?"

"Something was stuck in his chest."

"A knife?" Dr. Arlington asked.

"No, no, not a knife," Mason said. "I think it was a much smaller pointed object."

"Not a nail?" Dr. Arlington said.

"Probably something about the size of an ice pick."

"I see."

"He probably won't give you any information about how it happened," Mason said, "although he may tell you that he was standing in front of the kitchen door when his wife came through with a big load of dishes, and kicked the door open. He was holding an ice pick in his hand, and the suddenly opened door jabbed it into his chest."

"Is that the way it happened?"

"He may tell you that's what happened."

"Did it happen that way?"

"How do I know?" Mason asked. "You go on up and find out what's wrong with the guy. He's having chills."

"The devil he is!"

"Uh-huh."

"That'd better be looked into," Dr. Arlington said. "An ice pick can be damned serious."

"All right," Mason told him. "Go look into it."

8

DR. ARLINGTON TOOK his professional bag, walked up to the door of the apartment house and pressed the button on 218.

A few moments later the buzzer sounded and Dr. Arlington pushed the door open and went in.

"Well," Mason said to Della Street, "we'll soon find out just how much of a problem we have. You got that ice pick placed all right?"

"I'll say I did. I put it in the utility drawer in the kitchen."

"You were working pretty fast," Mason told her.

"You gave me a wonderful opportunity, inquiring about the woman's marital status. Wasn't that rather mean, Chief?"

"It was a good way to keep her attention occupied," Mason said.

"You didn't need to rub it in! She'll know what's in the apartment and, when she finds that extra ice pick, particularly since the price mark was left on it, she'll know it was planted and then she'll put two and two together."

Mason said, "And again she may feel that the ice pick with a price tag still on it *must* have been the one used in the stabbing."

Della Street thought that over for a moment, then smiled. "I think I begin to see a light," she said, "a very interesting and significant light."

Mason lit a cigarette. "We'll see what they tell Dr. Arlington."

"Don't you think you should have gone up with him?"

Mason said, "I don't want to be a witness. Let Dr. Arlington talk with the guy. Any court in the land will take Dr. Arlington's testimony at face value."

"I'll say," she agreed. "He makes a fine witness."

Della Street, who was standing by the side of Perry Mason's automobile, looking toward the back of the car, suddenly stiffened to attention, said, "Oh-oh, Chief! Here's trouble!"

"What?" Mason asked.

"A very official-looking car with a red spotlight."

"Coming here?" Mason asked.

"Looks like it."

"Jump in," Mason told her. "We'll get going. We don't dare to get caught—"

"There's not time," she interrupted. "They're right on us. Make up a good story."

"Get in," Mason said, sliding over so Della could get in behind the steering wheel. "They may not notice you."

Della Street, with quick, supple grace, twisted in behind the steering wheel, slammed the door shut, rolled the window down.

"Act as though you hadn't seen them," Mason said,

"and be talking. They probably won't notice a parked car. They—"

He broke off as the interior of the car was flooded with red light from a police spotlight.

"Turn around," Mason said. "Look surprised! Otherwise they'll know we had seen them coming."

Mason turned quickly, then faced Della Street and said, "Look, look!" He pointed back toward the spotlight.

"How's that, Della?" he asked.

"Corny, but good," she said. "Here they are."

Sgt. Holcomb of Homicide Squad came walking up on the right side of the car. An officer moved up to the left-hand side.

"Well, well, well," Sgt. Holcomb said. "What are *you* doing here?"

"And what in the world are *you* doing here?" Mason asked. "We were just leaving."

"Were you really!" Holcomb said. "It didn't look like it to me. It looked as though you were waiting for someone. You know, Mason, you shouldn't have such an attractive secretary. When you get a girl with a figure like Miss America . . ."

"Miss Universe," Mason interrupted, grinning.

"All right, all right," Holcomb said with the easy good nature of one who has trumped all the aces in the deck. "When you get a good-looking secretary with a figure like Miss Universe, we naturally notice her when she slides in behind the steering wheel of an automobile. Now, suppose you tell me just *what* you're waiting for?"

Della Street, looking toward the door of the apartment house, nudged Perry Mason.

Dr. Arlington came hurrying out, took a step toward Mason's car, then seeing the officers, veered over toward his own car.

Holcomb watched him with smiling amusement.

"Oh, Doctor," he called.

Dr. Arlington stopped, looked back over his shoulder, said, "Yes?"

"You *are* a doctor, aren't you?" Sgt. Holcomb asked, staring pointedly at the medical bag.

"Yes."

"May I ask where you've been, Doctor?"

"In that apartment house," Dr. Arlington said.

"Wonderful!" Sgt. Holcomb observed. "Since we saw you come out of the apartment house, I have no reason to doubt your statement. Now, could you be a little more specific, Doctor, and tell us just what apartment you were in, in that house?"

"I fail to see that it concerns anyone," Dr. Arlington said.

"Oh, but I think it does," Sgt. Holcomb observed. "If you were up in Apartment 218, it would be of the greatest concern to the police. And if you were sent there by Mr. Perry Mason, then the situation would be more than interesting. It would be downright exciting.

"The fact that Mr. Mason was quite apparently waiting for you to come out indicates that he knew you were in there. If he knew you were in there, the probabilities are that he was responsible for you being there. The fact that you started to walk toward Mr. Mason's car as though to make a report to him, then saw the police car parked behind and made a sudden swing over to the car which, I take it, is your car, was quite a giveaway. What did you find, Doctor?"

Dr. Arlington reached a quick decision. He smiled and said, "I was making a checkup on a person who had been injured. I assumed it was a civil case with the possibility of malingering."

He looked past the officer standing by the side of the car to Perry Mason, raised his voice and said, "The man was dead by the time I got there. The woman who was with him, and who I assume is his wife, gives a history of an ice pick having been inserted in the man's chest. I made a quick examination and convinced myself that there had indeed been a small puncture wound in the chest. Under the circumstances, I felt that it was a case for the coroner and did nothing further."

"You called the police?" Sgt. Holcomb asked.

"The police had been called *before* I arrived," Dr. Arlington said. And then, with a meaning glance at Perry Mason, said, "I would, of course, have notified the coroner if the young woman hadn't already called the authorities."

"That's most interesting," Sgt. Holcomb said. "Now perhaps someone will tell us how it happened that Mr. Mason knew this man had been injured."

Mason said, "Just a moment, Doctor. Was there anyone in the apartment when you left?"

"Just the young woman."

"Do you know whether she's his wife?"

"I don't know. How should I? I didn't ask to see the marriage license."

"In other words, then, she's up there alone with the body and any evidence that may be in the apartment."

"That is correct," Dr. Arlington said.

Sgt. Holcomb sighed. "All right, Mason," he said, "you win. Much as I would like to interrogate you, I realize that my first duty is to get up there and investigate the homicide."

"Homicide?" Mason asked. "Wasn't it accidental?"

Sgt. Holcomb grinned. "The story we got over the telephone is that some woman pushed an ice pick right into his chest. However, we'll find out a lot more about it. Don't go away, Mason."

"Why not?" Mason asked.

"I'm going to want to talk with you."

"You can talk with me at my office."

"I don't want to waste the time," Sgt. Holcomb said. "I'm not going to detain you any longer than necessary, but you and the doctor stay right here. Now, let me ask you, have you been up in that apartment, Mason?"

"Yes," Mason said.

"That's what I thought."

"You want me with you, Sergeant?" the other officer asked.

"I want you with me," Holcomb said. "Another car with a deputy coroner and a fingerprint man will be here any minute."

He turned to Mason. "I'm giving you a lawful order from an officer in the performance of his duty. Don't leave here until I have a chance to talk with you."

Mason said, "All right, if it's a *reasonable* order, I'll obey it. But it has to be reasonable. I'll give you fifteen minutes. That's a reasonable length of time. If you have any questions you want to ask me or Dr. Arlington here, be back inside of fifteen minutes."

"I've a job of investigation to do up there."

"You can get the woman out of the apartment, seal up the apartment so that nothing will be touched," Mason said, "and you can do all that within two minutes. You'll have ten minutes for a first investigation and then you can come down here and talk with me. At the end of fifteen minutes I'm going to be on my way, and Dr. Arlington is going to be on his way."

Sgt. Holcomb hesitated a moment, then turned to the officer. "Come on, let's go!" he said.

When they had gone, Dr. Arlington said in a low voice to Perry Mason, "I didn't know what to do, Perry. The man was dead when I arrived. He evidently had been dead for about ten minutes."

"How about the woman with him. Hysterical?"

"Upset. . . . But I wouldn't think he was irreplaceable in her life."

"Did she tell you anything I should know?" Mason asked.

"Only that she'd telephoned the officers. She said she told them Carl Harrod had been murdered."

"Murdered?"

"That's what she said: murdered. I was in a spot, Perry. I didn't know what you wanted; whether I should dash back down here and tell you that the man was dead and that she had called the authorities, or whether I should take a quick look at the body so I could see the nature and location of the wound.

"I decided you'd want to know something about the wound, so I pulled back the blankets and took a look. There was a small, livid puncture wound, and, unofficially, I have no doubt it was made with an ice pick and that it was the cause of death."

"Just one wound?" Mason asked.

"Just one wound. Of course, I didn't examine the entire body, but the man was naked from the waist up. I'm quite certain there was just that one puncture wound, at least in the chest cavity."

"All right," Mason said wearily. "We seem to be in a hell of a spot right now. Della, I think you'd better go telephone our client. . . . Hold it," Mason said sharply, as she placed her hand on the door latch, "here comes an officer to ride herd on us until it suits Sgt. Holcomb to come down and give us the third degree."

The officer who had gone up with Sgt. Holcomb came back from the apartment house, started across the sidewalk.

A second police car rounded the corner. The driver was unable to find a parking place, so double-parked with the red blinker on the top of the car flaring vivid flashes of warning light.

Men hurried from the car. A photographer carrying a heavy camera case by means of a shoulder strap, a smaller camera in one hand and a Strobe-light in the other hand, hurried across to the apartment house. He was followed by an officer carrying a fingerprint camera and a small, black case of the sort used to carry materials for developing latents.

The officer who had come down from the apartment moved over to confer with the newcomers briefly.

Two more men debouched from the second police automobile and entered the apartment house.

The officer came over to stand by Mason's car.

"Sgt. Holcomb says he doesn't want to detain you unduly, but he does want to question you and he doesn't want any of you to drive away."

"I'm a doctor," Dr. Arlington said. "I can't neglect my patients. I have to be where I can be available for phone calls and—"

"I know, I know," the officer interrupted. "It won't be long."

"Fifteen minutes from the time Sgt. Holcomb spoke to us," Mason said, "is a reasonable time. I advise you, Doctor, that if you are not interrogated and released within fifteen minutes, you are legally within your rights in leaving."

"Now, wait a minute," the officer said. "You can't pull that stuff. The law doesn't say anything about fifteen minutes."

"The law requires that any police order must be reasonable," Mason said. "Under the peculiar circumstances of this case, I feel that fifteen minutes is a reasonable time. I'm willing to accept that responsibility."

"Well, you may be accepting a hell of a lot of responsibility," the officer warned roughly.

"In my business I'm accustomed to accept a hell of a lot of responsibility," Mason told him.

The officer was plainly uneasy. He glanced anxiously at the door of the apartment house. "The sergeant said to hold you until he got here."

"I tell you I'm leaving in fifteen minutes."

"You're leaving when the sergeant says you can leave."

"I'm leaving in fifteen minutes from the time he told us to wait," Mason snapped.

The officer was trying to think of the answer to that, when the door opened and Sgt. Holcomb came striding across the sidewalk and out to the car.

"So," he said, "you and Miss Street got a statement from the guy and Della Street took it down in shorthand."

"Right," Mason said.

"He was stabbed by a client of yours."

"Wrong," Mason said.

"How the hell do you know?" Sgt. Holcomb asked.

"My clients don't stab people."

"Well," Sgt. Holcomb said, "it seems that the stabbing was done by a woman who was in the apartment occupied by Fern Driscoll, 309 at the Rexmore Apartments. Is Miss Katherine Baylor a client of yours, Mason?"

"I've never seen her in my life."

"How about Fern Driscoll?"

"Fern Driscoll is my client."

"All right. I'm going to see her. What's more, I want to see her before you have a chance to do any telephoning."

Sgt. Holcomb looked at his watch. "You hold them here for ten minutes," he said to the officer, "and then you can let them go. However, I'm going to want to hear from you, Mason. I want a statement from you and I want a copy of the statement that this man Harrod made as to the circumstances surrounding the stabbing."

"How about the doctor?" the officer asked.

"Don't let anybody get to a phone for ten minutes," Sgt. Holcomb said. "I want to get up to that apartment and talk with this Driscoll woman before Mason has a chance to tip her off to clam up and say nothing. As I see it, she's the most valuable witness we are going to find."

Mason said, "I'm afraid, Sergeant, you don't understand how I work."

"I know all about how you work," Holcomb told him.

"Keep them here, Ray. In exactly ten minutes you may let them go."

Sgt. Holcomb hurried away.

Mason looked at his wrist watch, stretched, yawned, lit a cigarette, put his head back against the cushion and closed his eyes.

Dr. Arlington, taking his cue from Perry Mason, went over to his car, opened the door and started to get in.

"Stay right here for ten minutes," the officer warned.

"Nine minutes now," Dr. Arlington said, climbing into his car and slamming the door shut.

Della Street, with an eye on her wrist watch, counted off the minutes.

"All right, Chief," she said, "nine and a half minutes."

At Mason's nod, she started the motor.

"Hold it," the officer said. "You have thirty seconds to go."

"Just warming the car up," Mason told him.

The officer seemed uneasy. "I'd like to get word from Sgt. Holcomb. He could communicate with us through communications and on the car radio."

"I know he could," Mason said, "but he said ten minutes, and ten minutes it is."

The officer seemed undecided.

"Okay, Della," Mason said.

Della Street, in the driver's seat, eased the car into gear.

Dr. Arlington's car slid out behind them.

"Now where?" Della asked.

"Drake Detective Agency," Mason said, "but first signal Dr. Arlington to come alongside."

Della Street drove for a block, then pulled off to the side of the road, motioned with her arm for Dr. Arlington to come alongside on the one-way street.

When Dr. Arlington was running abreast Mason said, "Go on home, Doctor, and don't answer questions."

Dr. Arlington nodded to show that he understood and shot ahead.

Della Street said, "I think Paul Drake is in the office tonight. He told me he was working on a case and expected to be there until nearly midnight."

"That's fine," Mason said. "We'll talk with Paul personally. Swing over to the right and turn a corner, Della. I presume that officer is still watching our tail-light and it's quite possible Sgt. Holcomb might relay a radio message to him asking him to hold us for another inquiry."

9

THE NIGHT SWITCHBOARD OPERATOR at the Drake Detective Agency offices looked up as Mason held the office door open for Della Street.

She nodded and smiled.

"Anybody in with Paul?" Mason asked.

"No, Mr. Mason, he's alone."

"Tell him we're on our way," Mason said.

The operator nodded and plugged in a telephone line.

Mason opened the gate which led to a corridor lined with doors opening into small cubbyhole offices.

Paul Drake's private office was at the end of the corridor.

Mason opened the door.

"Hi, Perry!" the detective said. "Hi, Della. What brings you out at this time of night?— Oh-oh, I'll bet I don't want to know the answer."

Mason pulled up a chair for Della Street, then sat

down next to Drake's desk. "Paul, we're mixed up in a case that I can't figure out. I want a lot of research work done and I want it done fast."

Drake picked up a pencil and moved a pad of paper toward him.

Tall, long-limbed, poker-faced, he moved with an easy, double-jointed rhythm which seemed awkward, yet eliminated all waste motion.

"Shoot!"

"A girl using the name of Fern Driscoll, 309 Rexmore Apartments. I want everything you can get on Fern Driscoll. She was working in Lansing, Michigan, and left suddenly. Now, this girl who's using Fern Driscoll's name has a job with the Consolidated Sales and Distribution Company."

"This floor?" Drake asked, looking up.

"This floor."

"I know the head of that concern pretty well," Drake said. "I can get a line on her."

"She's only been here ten days or two weeks. I want to get her background."

"Okay, anything else?"

"Harriman Baylor of Lansing. A big-shot manufacturer. A daughter named Katherine and a son named Forrester. I want everything you can get on the family. Fern Driscoll worked for Baylor's company in Lansing."

"That's all?"

"Carl Harrod of the Dixiecrat Apartments, 218. I want to know everything about his past."

"How about the present?" Drake asked.

"There isn't any," Mason told him.

Drake looked up sharply. "What do you mean?"

"It's all in the past," Mason explained.

"Since when?"

"Probably about an hour ago."

"All of this is going to take lots of men and lots of time," Drake told him.

"It's going to take lots of men and probably lots of money, but it can't take lots of time."

"Why?"

"Because we don't have that much time."

"Do the police know about Harrod?"

"Yes."

"About your interest in him?"

"Hell yes!" Mason said. "I got caught standing in front of the apartment waiting for Dr. Arlington to come down and make a report."

"Report on what?"

"Nature and extent of the injuries. He was stabbed with an ice pick. The woman who was living with Harrod had already called headquarters before we got there and reported the death as a homicide. My friend, Sgt. Holcomb, caught me flat-footed."

"So what happens next?" Drake asked.

"I don't know," Mason said. "I want all the information I can get before the going begins to get tough."

"I take it there's some sort of a tie-in by which all of these people are joined together more or less?"

"There may be," Mason said.

"Okay. Where are you going now?"

"Down to my office," Mason told him. "You start getting information, relay it in as fast as you can get it. Minutes may be precious. We're probably one jump ahead of the police on certain phases of the case and I'd like to keep ahead of them as far as possible.

"The Baylor family use the Vista del Camino Hotel as headquarters. They're very shy about the wrong sort of publicity. Carl Harrod was all set to see that they got lots of it.

"Katherine Baylor is in town. She may be implicated in some way. On the other hand, the girl using the name of Fern Driscoll says *she* did the stabbing."

"You don't think this girl is really Fern Driscoll?"

"I *know* she's Mildred Crest of Oceanside. Get busy and check everything."

"Okay," Drake said, "get down to your office and let me start pouring instructions into the telephone. I'll have ten men on the job within ten minutes and each one of those men will put out more men if he has to."

Mason nodded to Della Street and they left Drake's office, walked down the corridor to Mason's office.

Mason latchkeyed the door, switched on the lights.

"Well?" Della Street asked, as Mason hung up his hat and settled back into a swivel chair.

"We wait it out—for a while at least," Mason said. "If our client is telling the truth, she was entirely within her rights in protecting herself."

"And if she's lying?"

"Then," Mason admitted, "things could be in quite a mess."

"She seems to have lied before."

"Exactly. Those lies are going to put her in quite a spot if the breaks start going against her.

"As Mildred Crest, she *could* find herself charged with the murder of Fern Driscoll. All that background of deceit is going to make her a pushover in this Harrod case—if the authorities decide it's murder."

They waited twenty minutes, then the unlisted phone rang sharply.

"I'll take it," Mason said. "It must be Paul Drake."

Mason picked up the receiver, said, "Hello, Paul."

Drake's voice came over the wire. "Get either morning paper. You'll find a picture of Harriman Baylor, the famous manufacturer and financial wizard, just getting off an airplane. He arrived late this afternoon. Reporters met him at the airport."

"I'll take a look," Mason said. "You say there's a photograph?"

"A nice photograph. Mr. Baylor is not out here on business. Mr. Baylor is out here for a well-earned vacation and for his health. Mr. Baylor has been troubled with bursitis."

"Bursitis, huh?" Mason said.

"Uh-huh. An infection of a capsule of fluid or something in the shoulder that—"

Mason laughed and said, "I know all about bursitis, Paul. That is, I know enough about it to cross-examine doctors. It can be stubborn and painful. We don't have our morning papers at the moment. Tell me, how did Mr. Baylor look in the photos?"

"Influential," Drake said. "He has many million dollars, and he looks like many million dollars. The photograph shows him holding a brief case in his left hand, his right hand waving his hat in greeting, a beautiful hostess on each side and a caption about the manufacturing and financial wizard who believes that the Pacific Coast is on the eve of an unprecedented growth. Baylor says that what has happened so far is merely scratching the industrial surface."

"Radiating optimism, eh?" Mason asked.

"Radiating optimism."

"Could I call him at the Vista del Camino Hotel?" Mason asked.

"No dice," Drake said. "Trying to get a phone call through to him requires an Act of Congress and the unwinding of yards of red tape. But he's there and, as nearly as I can find out, he's in his suite."

"What about his background, Paul?"

"Big manufacturer. Big financier. Big investor. Boards of directors and all that stuff. *Who's Who* takes a whole column on him."

"Find out anything about Katherine Baylor?" Mason asked.

"Postgraduate work at Stanford. Nice kid. Popular. For herself and not for her money. Unostentatious. A good scout. Something of a crusader, imbued with the idea of improving the administration of justice, safeguarding justice for rich and poor alike. A nice kid."

"Entanglements?"

"Apparently not. Nothing formal. Very popular, therefore it's hard to tell whether she's playing the field or has her eye on some particular individual. Apparently, there was an affair back East, something that the folks were afraid might prove serious, and that's the reason for postgraduate work at Stanford.

"I'm just beginning to get the dirt, Perry, and I'll have more for you in a little while. But in the meantime I thought you'd like to know about Baylor."

"That's fine," Mason said. "Keep digging and keep in touch with us. I think I'll go out to the Vista del Camino Hotel and try for an interview."

"No chance," Drake said. "He had a press interview at the plane, then he ordered everything shut off. No phone calls, no interviews. Nothing."

"Any exceptions?" Mason asked.

"I don't know. The house dick over there is a friend of mine. I might be able to find out."

"Find out and call me back," Mason said. "I'm interested."

The lawyer hung up the phone and Della Street drew a cup of coffee from the electric percolator.

"Listen in on the extension?" Mason asked.

She nodded.

"Take notes?"

Again she nodded.

Five minutes later Drake again called on the unlisted telephone.

"Now look, Perry," he said, "you're going to have to protect me on this. I got it from my close friend, the house detective. It would cost him his job if anyone knew there had been a leak coming from him."

"Go ahead," Mason said.

"Baylor has shut off all telephone calls. Everything.

His suite is completely isolated. There's even a guard at the door. He has, however, left instructions that if a Mr. Howley tries to get in touch with him, the call is to be put through immediately, no matter what hour of the day or night."

"Howley, eh?" Mason asked.

"That's right."

"Who's Howley, do you know?"

"Can't find a thing in the world about him. All I know is Baylor is sewed up tight except for Howley. And Howley is to be put through the minute he picks up a phone."

"Is Howley arriving at the hotel?" Mason asked.

"I don't know. Instructions are for action the minute Howley shows up. I gather that he's probably coming in on a plane or something and Baylor is waiting for him."

"But you don't have anything definite on that? That's just a hunch?"

"Hunch, hell! It's a deduction," Drake said.

"All you have is the deduction?"

"That's right."

"Why should Baylor be taking all those precautions?" Mason asked. "It would seem to indicate that he expects to become the center of interest somehow."

"He *is* a center of interest," Drake said. "He's a big shot."

"But he doesn't ordinarily take all those precautions against disturbance?"

"He doesn't ordinarily have bursitis and—probably he's working on a big business deal. I don't know. All I can do is get the facts and relay them to you. You're going to have to do your own thinking."

"No more deductions?" Mason asked.

"Not after the cool reception I got on the other one."

Mason laughed. "Don't be so sensitive. Keep working, Paul."

Mason hung up the telephone, looked at Della Street thoughtfully, said, "Try to reach our client, Della. Perhaps the police haven't taken her out of circulation. In that event, they've probably completed their questioning and we might be able to get her on the line."

Della Street put through a call, got no answer, so called the manager of the apartment house, asked for Fern Driscoll in Apartment 309, said, "Just a moment, please," then turned to Mason. "The manager says Miss Driscoll left with two men and asked the manager to hold all mail."

"Okay," Mason said, "hang up."

Della Street said, "Thank you. I'll call later," and hung up.

Suddenly Mason turned to his secretary. "You sit here and hold the fort, Della. I'm going over to the Vista del Camino Hotel."

"Be careful," she warned.

Mason nodded.

Mason left the office and went directly to the Vista del Camino Hotel.

In the lobby the lawyer picked up one of the room phones, said, "Connect me with Mr. Harriman Baylor, please."

"I'm sorry, but Mr. Baylor's phone has been temporarily disconnected. He has left orders that he's not to be disturbed."

"Well, he'll talk with me," Mason said. "I'm supposed to call him."

"I'm very sorry, but there are to be absolutely no— Just a moment. What's the name, please?"

"Howley," Mason said.

Mason heard the sound of swift whispers, then the operator said, "Just a moment, Mr. Howley. If you'll hold on, I'll see if we can get Mr. Baylor."

A few moments later a rich baritone voice said cautiously, "Hello. This is Harriman Baylor speaking."

"Howley," Mason said.

Baylor's voice showed excitement. "Where are you now?"

"In the lobby."

"Well, it's about time," Baylor said. "They had the damnedest report that you'd been— Wait a minute. How do I know you're Howley?"

"As far as that's concerned," Mason said, "how do I know you're Baylor?"

"What's your other name, Howley?"

"Look," Mason said, "I'm not going to stand down here in the lobby where anyone can buttonhole me at any minute and have you give me a catechism. I'll come up there, then I'll answer your questions. I—"

"What's the other name I know you by?" Baylor interrupted.

Mason hesitated.

Suddenly the receiver clicked at the other end of the line and the line went dead.

Mason immediately left the room phone, sauntered across the lobby to the cigar stand and waited.

A house detective hurried to the bank of house phones, looked around, then made a survey of the lobby.

Mason lit a cigarette, strolled over to one of the reclining chairs, settled back and waited.

A bellboy, closely followed by the house detective, paged "Mr. Howley."

Mason made no move. He waited for five minutes, then went to the hotel drugstore, entered a phone booth and again called the number of the Vista del Camino Hotel.

"Will you please tell Mr. Harriman Baylor," Mason told the operator who answered, "that Mr. Howley is calling?"

The operator hesitated perceptibly, then after a moment a man's voice came on the line.

"Hello?" the voice asked.

"Mr. Baylor?" Mason asked.

"That's right," the voice said.

"Howley," Mason told him.

"Where are you now, Mr. Howley?"

"Not too far away," Mason said.

"If you tell me where you are, I'll—"

"Look here," Mason said indignantly, "this isn't Baylor. Who the hell is that?"

"Now, just a minute! Take it easy! Take it easy!" the man's voice said. "We're filtering Mr. Baylor's calls. Someone tried to get through to him by using your name. Just a minute, and I'll put Baylor on."

A moment later another voice came on the line. "Hello," the voice said cautiously.

"Baylor?" Mason asked.

"Yes."

"Howley."

Baylor said promptly, "What was the other name you gave me, Howley?"

"Why, hell! *You* know," Mason said.

"I know," Baylor retorted. "But I want to be sure that this is the man I think it is. What was the other name?"

"Carl Harrod," Mason said promptly.

"All right," Baylor told him, relief in his voice, "that's better! There was a report around that you were seriously incapacitated, that— Never mind, I'll discuss that with you. Now, I want you to come up to my suite. It's the presidential suite, Suite A. But you can't get near the door of the suite because it's guarded. Walk up to Room 428 and knock on the door. Knock twice, wait a moment, knock twice more, then wait a moment, and knock once. Do you understand that?"

"Perfectly!" Mason said.

"All right, I'll see you there. How long will it take you to get there?"

"About two minutes," Mason told him.

"Did everything go all right?"

"Everything went fine."

91

"All right. Come on up and we'll discuss arrangements."

Mason hung up the telephone, sauntered into the hotel, took the elevator to the fourth floor, walked down the corridor. Presidential Suite A was at the end of the corridor, and the entrance was blocked by a man who was over six feet tall, bullnecked, and built like a wrestler.

The man eyed Mason suspiciously. Mason paid no attention to him but turned sharply to the left to the door of 428 and knocked twice, waited a moment, knocked twice more, waited another moment, then knocked again.

The door was opened by a stocky, quick-moving individual in the early fifties, a man with a high forehead, bushy eyebrows, dark piercing eyes, and an assertive manner.

He recoiled as he saw Mason. His left hand holding the doorknob tried to slam the door shut.

Mason lowered his shoulders, pushed the door open and walked into the room.

"I'm Perry Mason, Mr. Baylor," he said. "I'm the attorney for the young woman in the Rexmore Apartments. I think you and I had better have a talk."

Baylor stepped back, said, "Perry Mason, the lawyer?"

"That's right."

Baylor said, "I'm sorry, but you can't come in, Mason. I can't see anyone!"

"Except Carl Harrod," Mason said. "For your information, Carl Harrod is dead."

"I . . . I . . ."

Mason kicked the door shut. "A great deal is going to depend on decisions you and I reach during the next few minutes, Mr. Baylor. I want to get some cards on the table."

"I don't want to talk with you. I've been warned about you."

Mason said, "I don't know how long you're going to have to discuss matters before the police get here. For your information, Mr. Baylor, I happen to know that Carl Harrod was blackmailing you. Carl Harrod was stabbed in the chest with an ice pick. He died a short time ago. He made a statement to me that Fern Driscoll had stabbed him with the ice pick, but under questioning admitted it could just as well have been your daughter Katherine that had pushed the ice pick into his chest.

"Now, I don't care how big you are or how powerful you are; Harrod's death is going to make complications. I don't know all the ramifications of what happened to Fern Driscoll, but it seems to me, you and I had better exchange a few facts before the newspapers come out with a sensational story."

"The newspapers!" Baylor exclaimed.

"Exactly," Mason said.

Baylor hesitated, suddenly said, "All right. You win!" He extended his left hand and shook hands with Mason. "You'll pardon the left hand," he said. "My bursitis has become suddenly worse. Come on in and we'll talk things over."

Baylor led the way across Room 428, which was fitted up as an ordinary hotel bedroom, through a connecting door and into the reception room of a luxurious suite.

"This is my daughter, Katherine," he said. "Katherine, this is Perry Mason, an attorney, who is representing Fern Driscoll."

Katherine Baylor jumped to her feet, her eyes wide with some emotion Mason was unable at the moment to classify. She moved over to give him her hand.

"Mr. Mason," she said.

"It's a pleasure to meet you," Mason said. And then added quietly, "My client has told me about you."

"Oh!" Kitty said.

"All right," Baylor said. "Sit down, Mason. Perhaps we'd better put some cards on the table."

Mason selected a chair, stretched his long legs out in front, crossed his ankles.

"Now, what's all this about Harrod having been killed?" Baylor asked.

"Stabbed with an ice pick," Mason said. "At first Harrod said Fern Driscoll had pushed the ice pick into his chest. Then it became clear that your daughter Katherine may have done it."

"What!" Katherine Baylor exclaimed. "Why, that's absolutely absurd! I slapped his face and—"

"Suppose you let Mr. Mason and me do the talking, Kitty," Harriman Baylor said. "I'd like to find out a little more about Mason's position in the matter, and exactly what it is he wants."

Mason said, "I want facts. I want to know exactly what your relations were with Harrod. I want to know why you came in here and closed off every means of communication providing that no one could reach you except Carl Harrod who was to call you under the name of Howley."

"And I want to know how *you* got *that* information," Baylor snapped.

Mason smiled. "I'm afraid there's some information I can't give you."

"Can't or won't?"

"Won't!"

"That's not a very good way to start playing your hand," Baylor said.

"It's my way," Mason told him.

Baylor colored. "I don't let men dictate to me, Mr. Mason."

"Probably not," Mason said. "However, we have one essential difference, Mr. Baylor."

"What's that?"

Mason grinned. "*I* don't care how often they put *my* name in the newspapers, and *I* don't care how large the type is."

Baylor's aggressive personality visibly collapsed.

"Precisely what do you want, Mason?"

"First," Mason said, "I want to know all about Fern Driscoll."

Baylor said, "There isn't any reason why you shouldn't know everything I know. Miss Driscoll was employed as my son's secretary. It is possible that some romantic attachment developed. It is even possible that Miss Driscoll was foolish enough to think a person in my son's position could have married her, and she may even have dared to think such an event would take place."

Mason regarded the man thoughtfully. "You say she *dared* to think that?"

"She may have."

"You consider such an event improbable?"

Baylor flushed and said, "I consider it utterly impossible!"

"May I ask why?"

"There are certain reasons that I don't think we need to go into at the present time, aside, of course, from the obvious difference in social status."

"You consider that important?" Mason asked.

"Quite important!" Baylor said drily.

The telephone rang. Evidently some sort of an agreed-upon signal: a long, two shorts and a long.

Katherine Baylor moved toward the phone, but her father shook his head, strode across the room, picked up the telephone, said impatiently, "Hello. Yes. What is it now?"

He listened for several seconds, then said, "Of course, I'll talk with him. Put him on!"

A moment later he said, "Hello, Sergeant. Yes, this is Harriman Baylor."

Again he listened for a few seconds, then said, "She is here with me. We will of course do everything in our power to co-operate, but any such charge as that is absolutely absurd! Now, I want to be certain of one thing: Are you positive that the man is dead?"

Baylor listened again for a few moments, then said: "I

am exceedingly busy at the moment. If you could come within . . . oh, say, half an hour, that would be more convenient. . . . I see. . . . Well, make it twenty minutes then. . . . I'm sorry, Sergeant, fifteen minutes is absolutely the best I can do for you . . . ! I'm sorry, but that's final. Fifteen minutes! I don't give a damn if you subpoena me before a thousand grand juries, I'm tied up for fifteen minutes . . . ! Very well. Good-by!"

Baylor slammed up the telephone, walked back to his chair, looked at his wrist watch, regarded Mason thoughtfully and said, "All right, Mason. We haven't time to do any more sparring for position.

"My son became involved with Fern Driscoll. She may be a most estimable young woman. I don't know. My son is also attached to a very nice young woman who is in his social set, a woman who would make him happy, and who could be unquestionably accepted into the social circle in which my son moves, something which would be exceedingly difficult for Miss Driscoll.

"Now then, the report seems to have spread in some way that there had been certain indiscretions; that Miss Driscoll was in trouble and that I had given her a large sum of money to leave town. That report is absolutely, unqualifiedly false."

"How about your son?" Mason asked.

"My son assures me that the report is false as far as he is concerned," Baylor said with dignity.

"Well," Kitty said, "I happen to know that—"

"That will do! Please keep out of this, Katherine," Baylor said. "The situation is rather delicate."

Kitty glanced indignantly at him. "What I was going to say might have been of some help. . . ."

"Please!" her father commanded.

She remained silent.

"Now then," Baylor went on, "the situation became complicated because of this man Harrod. It seems that Fern Driscoll was involved in some way in an automobile accident, and Harrod was an investigator for an insurance company. He started backtracking and somehow or other found out a lot of garbled facts. Somebody gave him a lot of misinformation. The point is that he was dealing with a scandal magazine, which he felt would pay him ten thousand dollars for the story."

"You talked with him?" Mason asked.

Baylor thought things over some four or five seconds, then said in the manner of a man who is weighing his words carefully, "I admit that I talked with him. Harrod seemed to feel that perhaps I would be willing to pay him an amount at least equal to that which he could receive from the magazine for the story. However, he evidently had been advised in some detail concerning the law of extortion and it was very difficult to get him to say *exactly* what he had in mind.

"Moreover, Mason, I am not a man who submits to blackmail.

"The reason I am telling you all of this is that, according to Harrod, Fern Driscoll had some rather indiscreet letters which my son had written, and my son has admitted to me that there is the possibility Miss Driscoll saved some of his letters. He is not entirely clear as to the contents of those letters.

"In view of my name and position, a scandal magazine would regard a story involving the family as a very choice tidbit. It would undoubtedly pay a top price for such a story, and the publication of that story would cause a very great deal of unfavorable comment in the circles in which I move."

Mason nodded.

Baylor looked at his watch, and suddenly increased the tempo of his words. "I only have a minute or two, Mr. Mason. I don't want the officers to find you here. A Sgt. Holcomb wants to interview my daughter concerning the death of this man Harrod."

Again Mason nodded.

"I take it you must know something about that?"

"Yes," Mason said.

"Do you know Sgt. Holcomb?"

"Yes."

"Well, I don't want Sgt. Holcomb to find you here, and I'm not going to tell Sgt. Holcomb that you have been here. I'm telling you all this very frankly, Mr. Mason. I wouldn't submit to blackmail. However, certain circumstances which now exist put me in a very embarrassing position. I have every reason to believe that Miss Driscoll may need first-class legal services. I think that Miss Driscoll has certain letters which my son wrote. I want those letters. When those letters are delivered to me, I am prepared to pay you in cash for representing Miss Driscoll."

"I'm not a blackmailer," Mason said.

"I don't want you to be a blackmailer. You're representing Fern Driscoll. Now then, you're going to have to do a great deal of legal work for her. She doesn't have the money to pay you the sort of fees you customarily get. I know a great deal about you by reputation.

"On the other hand, Miss Driscoll isn't a blackmailer and you're not a blackmailer. You wouldn't think of using those letters in any adverse way. However, Mr. Mason, let me point out to you the extreme danger of the situation. If the police should search Miss Driscoll's apartment and should find those letters, it is almost certain that even if the letters themselves don't find their way into the public press, the existence of those letters would be established and that would be enough to give this scandal magazine all of the verification it needed so that it could go ahead and publish this dastardly story.

"Therefore, without in any way being guilty of any extortion, without you being guilty of any unprofessional conduct, you can assure your client that, if she will turn over those letters to you, and you can give them to me, she can have your services and they will be fully paid for. Do I make myself clear?"

Mason nodded.

"But, Dad," Kitty said, "she *isn't* Fern Driscoll!"

Her father turned on her angrily. "I asked you please to keep out of this!"

Mason regarded Harriman Baylor thoughtfully.

"All right," Baylor said, "suppose she isn't Fern Driscoll. Suppose your client should even be an impostor. The situation then becomes even more delicate. If it should appear that Fern Driscoll was the woman who was killed, if the autopsy showed that she was in the second month of pregnancy, if she left my employ suddenly, pulling up her roots and leaving without even pausing to say goodby to her friends—and then if it should appear that she had letters from my son— Damn it, Mason! I don't have to draw *you* a blueprint! I don't have to point out anything that's as obvious as the nose on your face. I want those letters!"

"And," Mason said, "the reason that you were not going to see anyone except Harrod is that Harrod assured you he would have those letters and could deliver them to you in return for a cash payment. Is that right?"

"I don't propose to be cross-examined by you or anyone else," Baylor said, "and I want you out of here before the police come. I've said everything I care to say."

Baylor got up, strode across to the door, held it open.

Mason said, "I think I appreciate your position, Mr. Baylor."

"You'll consider my offer?"

"I'll consider the best interests of my client."

"You understand what I am trying to forestall?"

"Perfectly."

"If this magazine can't get some corroborating evidence, it won't dare to go ahead. If it can get the faintest bit of corroboration, it will come out with a story that will start a social scandal which will have a most disastrous effect.

"You need money for your services. I've told you how you can get an adequate fee."

"I understand you perfectly," Mason said. "I'll do whatever is best for my client."

He walked out.

10

MASON LATCHKEYED THE DOOR of his private office, grinned at Della Street, and said, "Well, we may as well go home."

"How did you come out?" Della Street asked.

"After making one false start, I got in to see Baylor. You may have one guess as to who Howley was."

"Howley?" she asked, puzzled. "Who was— Oh, I remember, Howley was the name Baylor gave the hotel telephone operators and the house detectives, the one person whose calls were to be put through and who was to be admitted to see him no matter what hour he called."

"That's right," Mason said. "Guess who Howley really was?"

"I give up, Chief. Who *was* Howley?"

"Howley," Mason said, "was the alias for Carl Harrod."

"Oh-oh!" Della exclaimed. And then after a moment, "How in the world did you ever find that out?"

"I took a chance," Mason explained. "I made a shot in

the dark. The first time I called up and said I was Howley, Baylor wanted to know under what other name he knew me, or words to that effect. He wasn't quite that crude, but he asked me what other name I had given him. I was hesitating, trying to think of some way out, when he slammed up the telephone.

"I thought things over for a while, came to the conclusion that Baylor was out here because of the Fern Driscoll situation, that Harrod had been in touch with him, that the situation was really crucial, that Harrod had probably given him some ultimatum and that Baylor was thinking it over.

"I had everything to gain and nothing to lose. So I went to another telephone, called once more, gave the name of Howley, and when Baylor again asked me under what other name he knew me, or words to that effect, I said 'Carl Harrod,' and that did the trick."

Della Street frowned. "Just what does that mean, Chief?"

"That," Mason said, "is something I'm trying to figure out. People should react to external stimuli in a manner consistent with their basic characteristics. Any time they don't *seem* to do so, it means that the external stimuli are being misconstrued by the investigator, or that the basic character of the person has been misconstrued or misinterpreted.

"Baylor puts up a bold front of being a man who will fight to the last ditch, a man who won't pay blackmail, a man who refuses to bow to anyone. Yet he flies out here from Michigan and, despite all of his bold protestations of independence, we find him making appointments with a blackmailer."

Mason started pacing the floor. He paced for several seconds, then spoke thoughtfully: "If it was part of the Fern Driscoll story, Harrod must have uncovered something new. He had approached Baylor in Michigan and intimated that he'd sell the story to Baylor for the same price that he could get from a magazine. Baylor threw him out."

Della Street said, "I can tell from the tone of your voice that, while you're thinking out loud, you have an idea what the answer is."

"The answer may be that Katherine Baylor has become involved in some way."

"How?" she asked.

"That," Mason said, "is one of the major mysteries of the case.

"And there again we run into inconsistent conduct. We know now that our client is actually Mildred Crest, that Fern Driscoll got in the car with Mildred and there was an accident. We know there's something phony about that accident. We know that Fern Driscoll died and Mildred took her identity, and yet the actions of Fern Driscoll aren't consistent."

"In what way?" Della Street asked.

"Fern Driscoll," Mason said, "was a pretty level-headed young woman. She was an executive secretary for Baylor's son in a big organization. She must have had responsibilities and executive capabilities. Then all of a sudden she goes completely haywire and does a lot of things that simply don't make sense, no matter how you look at them."

"An unmarried woman who finds herself pregnant can go completely haywire," Della Street said. "Just realize the situation in which she found herself."

"I'm trying to," Mason said, "but it still doesn't account for her actions. . . . Call Paul Drake, Della. Tell him I'm back and that we're closing up shop. See if he knows anything new."

Della Street put through the call, then said, "Paul says he has some red-hot information. He's coming right down."

Mason moved over to the door of his private office,

and as soon as he heard Drake's code knock, let the detective in.

"Well, how's it coming?" Mason asked.

"In bunches," Drake said. "I think your client's in one hell of a mess."

"Shoot!" Mason told him.

"According to Harrod's widow, Harrod made *another* statement after you left. This statement was when he realized death was imminent."

"Go ahead," Mason said, "what was the second statement?"

"The second statement was that your client is a complete impostor, that she's Mildred Crest of Oceanside, that Mildred's boy friend embezzled some money and skipped out, that Mildred picked up Fern Driscoll as a hitchhiker, that either there was an accident, in which Fern Driscoll was killed and Mildred decided to take her identity, or that Mildred deliberately killed Fern Driscoll in order to have another identity."

"Go ahead," Mason said tonelessly. "What else?"

"Fern Driscoll had been engaged in a red-hot romance with Forrester Baylor. Young Baylor told her he was going to marry her. It wasn't until she found herself pregnant that she realized young Baylor was completely under the domination of his father. Then the old man moved in, told Fern Driscoll she could never hope to get into the sacred social precincts of the Baylor family, gave her a chunk of money, and told her to get out.

"She got out, but she had with her a bunch of torrid letters in the handwriting of Forrester Baylor. She never intended to use those letters, but when Harrod started investigating Mildred Crest's automobile accident on behalf of the insurance carrier, and tried to find out the identity of the hitchhiker Mildred had picked up, he did a good job of it and unearthed the scandal.

"Since that didn't have anything to do with Harrod's job as an insurance investigator, he was willing to play it on the side for what it was worth. He intended to sell the story to a scandal magazine. He evidently offered the story to the editors, who became terribly excited about it. They told Harrod that they'd pay him ten thousand bucks for the story but that they'd require some sort of proof. In order to get that proof, Harrod decided he needed the letters young Baylor had written.

"Harrod started out trying to make a deal with Mildred Crest, who was posing as Fern Driscoll, in order to get the letters. He went up to see her and came to the conclusion she wasn't Fern Driscoll. On his second visit, he ran into Katherine Baylor in the apartment.

"So Harrod waited and paid a third visit to the apartment. That time someone jabbed an ice pick into his chest.

"He came home, grinning from ear to ear. He telephoned Baylor and they had some mysterious conversation. Then he called you.

"Now, here's the funny thing. When Harrod *first* came home, he told his wife Katherine Baylor had stabbed him. After he had this conversation over the phone with Baylor, he told his wife it was Mildred Crest who had stabbed him. He told her to get you on the line and that he was going to make you jump through hoops.

"After he talked with you, he told his wife he had to set the stage and pretend the injury was very serious. So he covered up with blankets.

"He was in great spirits until just before you came. Then he began to complain of feeling cold. He said he was having a chill when you were there and his wife thought that was all part of the act. After you left she knew he really was feeling bad. She suggested he get up and get into a hot bath. He started to do that, then gave an exclamation of pain, fell back in the chair, and died within five minutes.

"Now then, Perry, here's something that's going to bother you: the police searched the apartment of your client and found four thousand bucks in nice, new hundred-dollar bills. According to police reasoning, that's the money that Fern Driscoll was given by either Harriman Baylor or by Forrester Baylor to go away and have her baby.

"In any event, it isn't money that Mildred Crest could have had legitimately. It's money that must have come from the purse of Fern Driscoll, the hitchhiker. Taking it from the purse constitutes larceny.

"Police are going to build up a case on the theory that Mildred Crest either murdered Fern Driscoll in order to take over her identity, or that she stole her identity along with all the money that was in Fern Driscoll's purse, that when Carl Harrod got on the trail and found out what was happening, she decided to silence Carl Harrod by sticking an ice pick in his chest.

"That makes a nice, neat, first-degree murder case."

"They've taken my client into custody?" Mason asked.

"She's in custody. I think they already have her identified from the thumbprint on her driving license as Mildred Crest. It's going to make one hell of a story, and you're right in the middle of it."

"All right," Mason said, "they've hit us with everything in the bag now. There's nothing we can do at the moment except go home and go to bed.

"Keep your men working, Paul, trying to stay abreast of the situation. I'll talk with my client in the morning and see how much she's told them. The fat's in the fire by this time."

"Will they let you talk with her?" Drake asked.

"They'll have to," Mason said. "Once they've booked her for murder, she's entitled to counsel. They won't even *try* to stop me. If she's booked, they'll have a red carpet spread out for me. They'll be very, very careful to see that she has all of her rights."

"And if she isn't booked by morning?" Drake asked.

"Then it means the district attorney's office doesn't feel

it has a case, and that it will be trying to tie up loose ends."

Drake said drily, "With Baylor's millions trying to keep his daughter's name out of it, I think you'll find they have a case."

"We'll know by ten o'clock in the morning," Mason said. "Go home and get some sleep, Paul."

11

FOLEY CALVERT, one of Hamilton Burger's more skillful trial deputies, arose to address Judge Marvin C. Bolton.

"Your Honor," he said, "this is the case of People vs. Mildred Crest, alias Fern Driscoll. She is charged with first-degree murder and this is the preliminary hearing. I wish to make a brief statement in order to explain the position of the prosecution and the reason for certain steps which will be taken by the prosecution. This statement is addressed to the Court solely for the purpose of showing the manner in which proof is to be submitted."

"Very well," Judge Bolton said. "You may make a statement and the defense may have an opportunity to reply to that statement if it desires."

"Thank you, Your Honor," Calvert said. "It is the theory of the prosecution that Mildred Crest, faced with social disgrace in Oceanside, decided to disappear; that, as a part of her scheme for disappearance, she intended to find some young woman of about her age and general appearance and substitute identities with that woman, killing the victim and leaving the body to be found under such circumstances that it would appear that Mildred Crest had died in an automobile accident."

"Just a moment," Judge Bolton interposed, "aren't you going rather far afield, Counselor? I am, of course, aware that this statement is addressed solely to the Court. However, if you rely upon that theory in *this* proceeding, then when you come to present your case before a jury, aren't you going to be faced with the fact that you are trying to introduce evidence of another crime, and that such evidence is based on surmise?"

"No, Your Honor," Calvert said. "We are prepared to argue the point. If the Court will bear with me a moment. It isn't the murder of Fern Driscoll, who was the young woman the defendant picked up as a victim, that furnishes the dominant motivation here. It is the fact that Carl Harrod, the decedent, was an investigator for an automobile insurance company and that his investigation disclosed the facts in the case which the defendant was trying to conceal. Therefore, it became necessary for the defendant to murder Carl Harrod, in order to carry out her scheme and keep from having the whole house of cards collapse.

"That, if the Court please, furnishes the motivation. The prosecution will show that motivation by competent evidence, of course."

"The defendant has not been charged with the murder of Fern Driscoll?" Judge Bolton asked.

"No, Your Honor."

"I take it that, if you had an airtight case— Well, the Court will make no comment on that. However, it is significant that she is not being prosecuted for *that* murder."

"She may well be prosecuted for that murder at a later date, Your Honor. I will state that she is already being charged with robbery in that she took four thousand dollars from the purse of Fern Driscoll."

"Four thousand dollars?" Judge Bolton asked.

"Yes, Your Honor."

"You didn't make that point in your original statement."

"Perhaps I overlooked that point, Your Honor. However, there is no question—that is, in the minds of the prosecution—there is no question but that this defendant took four thousand dollars from the purse of Fern Driscoll after the death of that young woman."

Judge Bolton looked at Mildred Crest with a complete lack of sympathy. "Evidence as to these matters will be introduced at this hearing?" he asked.

"Yes, Your Honor."

"Does the defense wish to make any statement?" Judge Bolton asked.

"No statement at this time, Your Honor," Perry Mason said.

"Very well, call your witnesses," Judge Bolton told the prosecutor. His voice had a note of cold finality.

Calvert put on a procession of minor witnesses: persons who had worked with Mildred Crest in Oceanside, who identified the defendant as being Mildred Crest; the chief of police of Oceanside who testified that Robert Joiner had been a fugitive from justice since the twenty-second day of the month, the day on which Mildred Crest had disappeared.

The manager of the bank testified as to the amount of money Mildred had drawn out of her account on the day of her disappearance.

Mildred's former employer testified as to the amount of salary she was receiving, the amount of the last pay check she had been given, the fact that she had announced her engagement to Robert Joiner, and that on the day of Robert Joiner's disappearance she had appeared in his office around two-thirty in the afternoon, white to the lips, and obviously ill, that he had commented on her personal appearance, and she had stated she was very sick, and he had sent her home.

Calvert's next witness was a member of the highway patrol, who testified as to the automobile accident. This witness identified photographs showing the position of the body. He testified as to all of the details concerning the accident, including tracks down the canyon showing that one person had left the overturned automobile.

"Cross-examine," Calvert said.

Mason said, "The automobile caught fire?"

"Someone set fire to the automobile," the officer said.

"How do you know the fire was set?" Mason asked.

"Because of the position and character of the fire."

"Just what do you mean by that?"

"When the car went off the road, it happened that a large, jagged rock caught the gasoline tank and wrenched it partially off. A big hole was torn in the tank and a large part of the gasoline was spilled at that point. When the car came to rest at the bottom of the steep incline, some of the gasoline from the tank had soaked the extreme rear of the car. It did not reach the front of the car. The ignition had been switched off. The lights had been switched off. Someone was alive and in the car at the time. The switches didn't turn themselves off. Since they were off, there was no way for the fire to have started other than through the agency of a match."

"Couldn't the impact of steel grinding against the rocks have caused a series of sparks?" Mason asked.

"Well . . . yes, I suppose so."

"And couldn't one of those sparks have touched off the gasoline?"

"Perhaps," the officer conceded. "But in this case we *know* that the fire was set by a match and that it was set by a second match, because we found a first match at the scene of the wreck; a paper match had been torn from a book of matches and had been used presumably for illumination."

"You found a paper match?" Mason asked.

"Yes, sir."

"You don't know when that paper match was placed there—of your own knowledge, do you?"

"Well, no. We assumed that it was—"

"Never mind your assumption," Mason said. "What do you *know?* Do you know that the match was struck at the time of the accident or immediately thereafter?"

"No, I don't know it of my own knowledge."

"It could have been left there from the day before, couldn't it?"

"Why would any person have struck a match at that particular place down at the bottom of that rocky canyon?"

"Don't question me," Mason said. "Answer *my* questions. For all you know, of your *own* knowledge, that match could have been left there from the day before the accident, couldn't it?"

The officer thought for a moment, then admitted reluctantly, "Yes, I suppose so."

"Now then," Mason said, "you have stated in your direct examination that the fire was put under control by the action of a passing motorist?"

"The fire in the car was controlled, yes, sir."

"Will you please tell me again just how that happened?"

"A motorist, coming along the road, saw the flames. He had a fire extinguisher in his car. As I have mentioned, the bulk of the gasoline had been spilled at a distance shortly after the car left the road where a big rock had partially wrenched the gasoline tank from the car and had torn a big hole in the tank. The motorist with his fire extinguisher, seeing a car at the bottom of the canyon, scrambled down to a point below the main part of the fire, directed his fire extinguisher on the fire in the automobile, and was able to bring that fire under control before the automobile had been completely consumed."

"Now, you mentioned in your direct examination that a suitcase was found which was the property of Fern Driscoll?"

"I didn't say it was the property of Fern Driscoll. I said that the initials 'F. D.' were on the suitcase and that subsequently we were able to trace it to the store which had sold it to Fern Driscoll, a store in Lansing, Michigan."

"If the Court please," Foley Calvert said, "I will stipulate that, as to the suitcase, the witness is testifying on hearsay evidence and it may go out."

"I'm making no objection," Mason said. "That, I take it, is a matter about which the authorities have satisfied themselves, and I see no reason for putting the state to the expense of proving this by showing the purchase itself. The witness, who is apparently somewhat biased but thoroughly competent, has stated what his investigation disclosed, and I have made no objection."

"We have the clerk who made the sale to Fern Driscoll here in court," Calvert said. "We have brought him from Lansing, Michigan."

"Very well, you may put him on later," Judge Bolton said. "There seems to be no objection on the part of the defense to the statement of this witness concerning the results of the police investigation. The Court will accept that statement for what it is worth. Proceed with your questioning."

"We have no further questions of this witness if the defense has finished its cross-examination," Calvert said.

"The defense is finished."

Calvert next put on the doctor who had performed the autopsy on the body, which he had at first assumed was that of Mildred Crest. He described the nature of the injuries, particularly an injury to the back of the head, a depressed skull fracture which, he said, could possibly have been made with a blunt instrument.

"Prior to the time of the automobile accident?" Calvert asked.

"Yes, sir."

"Immediately prior to the time of the automobile accident?"

"Yes, sir."

"Have you reached any conclusion as to the sequence of events leading to the death of the person whom you examined under the mistaken assumption that the body was that of Mildred Crest?"

"Yes, I have."

"What is that event sequence?"

"I believe that the injury to the back of the head was sustained *before* the wounds which were received on the front of the face and which made the face virtually unrecognizable. I believe that death ensued before the burns which were on the body of the deceased."

"Cross-examine," Calvert said.

Mason studied the witness for a moment, then asked, "You subsequently learned that the body was that of Fern Driscoll, and was not the body of Mildred Crest?"

"I did. Yes, sir."

"Now then, the depressed fracture in the back of the head, which you have mentioned and which you feel could have been an injury which was incurred before the automobile accident: do I understand you to mean that this injury could have been inflicted with a weapon?"

"It is *exactly* the type of injury which would have been inflicted with a round bar of some sort."

Mason said, "The photographs of the accident show the body on the right-hand side of the car with the head and shoulders partially protruding from the opened door?"

"Yes."

"Indicating that the person had opened the car door and started to jump out?" Mason asked.

"I wouldn't say as to that."

"How could the position of the body be accounted for otherwise?"

"The body could have been deliberately placed in that position."

"You mean," Mason said, "that some person, and I take it you have in mind the defendant, could have partially opened the door of the car, held the head and part of the shoulders of Fern Driscoll out of the car with one hand while driving over the bank with the other?"

"That could have been done. Yes, sir."

"Holding a body half-in and half-out of the car with the right hand, driving the car with the left hand?"

"It could have been done."

"It would have taken a great deal of strength?"

"It might have."

"And would have necessitated the driver of the car remaining in the car while it plunged down the deep canyon?"

"Yes."

"What assurance, then, did the driver have that she wouldn't be killed or seriously injured in the plunge?"

The witness hesitated. "Quite naturally, she couldn't have had any assurance at all."

"The bank was so steep that it was rather unusual for one of the persons in the car to be uninjured?"

"It was *very* unusual, almost miraculous."

"Then what would have been the motive for the defendant to have killed Fern Driscoll and held her body partially out of the car, if the probabilities were the defendant would also be killed?"

"If the Court please, that's argumentative," Calvert objected.

Judge Bolton smiled. "It *is* argumentative, but this witness, as an expert, has given reasons for his conclusions which give counsel the right to question his conclusions. The objection is overruled. Answer the question, Doctor."

The witness pursed his lips, shifted his position in the witness chair. "Of course, I can't duplicate the defendant's reasoning. She may well have contemplated suicide."

"Then the murder of Fern Driscoll would have done her no good?"

The witness squirmed uncomfortably. "That, I believe, is obvious."

"Now," Mason went on, "assuming that the decedent, whom you autopsied, had become panic-stricken when the car started to go over the grade and had jerked open the door on the right-hand side of the car trying to get out, would the position of the body, under those circumstances, have been the same as that of the body shown in this photograph?"

"Well . . . it could have been."

"And if the decedent had done that," Mason said, "isn't it possible that the doorpost of the automobile could have struck the back of her head at the first impact and left a depressed fracture exactly such as you have described?"

"Well . . . I don't know."

"Of course, you don't know," Mason said. "You've testified to a whole series of surmises. Now, I'm asking you if it isn't possible that the injury could have been sustained in that manner."

"It is possible, yes."

"And isn't it equally possible, as far as anything that *you* know of your *own* knowledge, from anything that you discovered at the autopsy, that the injury could just as well have been caused in that manner as by a blow inflicted with a round bar?"

"Well . . . perhaps."

"Yes or no?" Mason asked.

"Yes," the harassed witness blurted.

"Thank you," Mason said, smiling. "That's all."

Calvert put on the stand the manager of the Consolidated Sales and Distribution Company, who testified that the defendant had applied for a position with him and had given her name as Fern Driscoll; that she had given the social security number of Fern Driscoll; that she had stated her place of residence was Lansing, Michigan; and had further stated that she had recently arrived in the city and was looking for work.

Mason asked no questions on cross-examination.

The manager of the apartment house testified that the defendant rented an apartment, giving the name of Fern Driscoll and showing a driving license and social security card in the name of Fern Driscoll.

Again there was no cross-examination.

"Call George Kinney," Calvert said.

George Kinney held up his right hand, was sworn, gave his place of residence as Lansing, Michigan, and was, it turned out, the cashier of the Baylor Manufacturing and Development Company. George Kinney was also a shrewd individual who listened carefully to questions and had apparently been coached by some astute attorney as to exactly what he was to say, and exactly what he was to refrain from saying.

"Were you acquainted with an employee of the Baylor Manufacturing and Development Company named Fern Driscoll?"

"I was. Yes, sir."

"How long had she been in the employ of the corporation?"

"Two years, approximately."

"When did she sever her connections with the company?"

"On the ninth of last month."

"At the time she severed her connections, did you give her any money?"

"Yes, sir."

"How much?"

"I gave her a check covering the amount of her wages and severance pay."

"Did you give her anything else?"

"No, sir."

"During the period of her employment, had you come to know Fern Driscoll personally?"

"Yes, sir."

"At the time she terminated her employment, did you discuss with her the fact that her action was rather abrupt, and did she then and there make a statement to you as to the reason she was leaving the company?"

"Objected to," Mason said. "Incompetent, irrelevant, and immaterial. Hearsay as far as this defendant is concerned."

"Sustained!" Judge Bolton snapped.

"Did you notice her appearance at that time?"

"I did."

"Was there anything unusual in her appearance?"

"Objected to as incompetent, irrelevant and immaterial. Not binding on the defendant," Mason said.

"I'll hear the testimony," Judge Bolton said. "I think that may be pertinent. In view of the contention of the prosecution, the objection is overruled."

Kinney said, "She was very shaken. She was very white. She undoubtedly had been crying. Her eyes were swollen and red."

"That's all," Calvert said.

"You say that you knew her rather intimately?" Mason asked.

"I knew her personally, yes."

"By the way," Mason asked, "did she own an automobile?"

"Yes, sir."

"Do you know what kind of car it was?"

"I'm not sure of the make of the car, but I think it was a Ford. It was, I believe, about three years old. She had recently purchased it secondhand."

"That car was registered in Michigan? It had Michigan license plates?"

"She lived in Michigan, purchased the car in Michigan, and drove the car in Michigan," Kinney said with polite sarcasm. "One would naturally assume it had Michigan license plates."

"Thank you," Mason said with elaborate politeness. "That's all."

"I have one further question which perhaps I should have asked on direct examination," Calvert said.

"Very well," Judge Bolton said. "Ask your question."

"Shortly prior to the time Miss Driscoll left your employ, did Mr. Forrester Baylor have you withdraw rather a large sum of money from the bank for him, and did you turn that money over to him in cash?"

"Objected to as incompetent, irrelevant and immaterial," Mason said.

"If the Court please," Calvert said, "I would like to show that, at the time she left Michigan, Miss Driscoll had a rather large amount of money in her purse. I have shown that the defendant could not possibly have acquired some four thousand dollars in addition to her own bank account and salary check by any legitimate means. I would like to be permitted to show by inference that Fern Driscoll received rather a large sum of money from Forrester Baylor."

"You intend to show that by inference?"

"It is the only way I can show it, Your Honor."

Judge Bolton shook his head. "The objection is sustained."

"If the Court please," Calvert insisted, "I feel that we are entitled to resort to circumstantial evidence to prove motivation for the death of Fern Driscoll, particularly as we intend to show that Carl Harrod had acquired all this information."

"You may resort to circumstantial evidence," Judge

Bolton said, "and draw logical inferences from it, but you can't establish the circumstantial evidence by inference."

"Very well," Calvert said, "I have no further questions of this witness."

"No further cross-examination," Mason said.

"Call your next witness," Judge Bolton said.

"Call Sgt. Holcomb," Calvert announced.

Holcomb took the witness stand, testified that he was a member of the Homicide Squad; that he had been so employed on the second of the month; that on that date he had been called to an apartment occupied by Carl Harrod; that the person who had called him had given her name as Nellie Harrod and had stated that she was the wife of Carl Harrod; that when he arrived there Carl Harrod was dead.

"Did you make a search of the apartment occupied by this defendant under the name of Fern Driscoll?"

"I did."

"Did you find any money in that apartment?"

"Yes."

"What did you find?"

"I found four hundred and thirty-six dollars in currency of various denominations, and then I found forty new one-hundred-dollar bills."

"No other money?"

"No other money."

"I may wish to recall Sgt. Holcomb later for other aspects of the case," Calvert said, "but I have no further questions in regard to this matter. You may cross-examine, Mr. Mason."

Mason said, "I have no questions."

Sgt. Holcomb left the stand.

Foley Calvert said, "If the Court please, I have one more witness I would like to put on before the noon adjournment. This witness will give you very brief testimony."

"Very well," Judge Bolton said, glancing at the clock.

"Miss Irma Karnes," Calvert called.

Irma Karnes, a rather thin, young woman with a prominent, pinched nose, small lips, and eyes which peered out through heavy-lensed glasses, came forward and took her seat on the witness stand.

"Your name is Irma Karnes? You reside here in this city?"

"Yes, sir."

"And were so residing on the second of this month?"

"Yes, sir."

"What was your occupation on the second of this month?"

"I was manager of the notions department in the Arcade Novelty Company."

"And where is the Arcade Novelty Company, with reference to the apartment occupied by the defendant, if you know?"

"About three and a half blocks."

"Are you open during the evening?"

"Yes, until eleven-thirty."

"Can you describe the nature of the business?"

"It is a varied business. There is a penny arcade, so called, with the peep-show type of entertainment. There are electric guns shooting at moving game and electric machine guns shooting at airplanes. In fact, there are a whole host of novelty machines. Then back in the arcade we keep a line of notions and novelties."

"Such as what?" Calvert asked.

"Bottle openers, ice picks, corkscrews, tumblers, plastic buckets for ice, thermal containers for ice cubes, needles, threads, buttons, neckties, shaving supplies, razor blades. In short, a whole list of notions and novelties of the kind persons might want to buy at night."

"You mentioned ice picks?"

"Yes, sir."

"Now, do you remember any transaction connected with ice picks on the second of this month?"

"Yes, sir. I do indeed."

"What was that transaction?"

"A young woman came in and bought three ice picks. As it happened, those were all of the ice picks we had on display in the little glass compartment where we keep the ice picks. After she had gone, I went to replace the stock and then found that we had only half a dozen ice picks left in stock."

"So what did you do then?" Calvert asked.

"Is this relevant to the case?" Judge Bolton asked.

"Quite relevant, Your Honor."

"Very well, go on. There seems to be no objection on the part of defense counsel. However, it would seem to me to be somewhat remote."

"It is simply for the purpose of making an identification, if the Court please."

"Very well. She may answer."

The witness said, "I put those six ice picks in the display stand. I took some Scotch tape and price tags, preparing to put price tags on the ice picks, but before I did so, I looked up the catalog number and put a gross of ice picks on our want list. It was then I discovered that there had been a paste-over in the catalog and that ice picks had gone up in price."

"So what did you do?"

"The other ice picks had been thirty-eight cents, three for a dollar. I found I would have to sell the new ice picks at forty-one cents straight, in order to keep our margin of profit, so I put the new price on those ice picks."

"And were some of those ice picks purchased that same evening while you were there in the store?"

"Yes, sir."

"Who purchased them?"

She pointed a long finger at Mildred Crest. "The defendant came in and purchased three ice picks."

"At the new price?"

"At the new price."

"And that new price was written on labels fastened to the ice picks and covered with transparent plastic tape?"

"Yes."

"And those were the three ice picks which were purchased by the defendant in this case?"

"Yes, sir."

"That is all. You may cross-examine," Calvert said.

"Just a moment," Judge Bolton announced. "It appears that it is time for the usual noon recess. Court will take a recess until two o'clock this afternoon. The defendant is remanded to custody."

12

PERRY MASON, DELLA STREET, and Paul Drake sat in the little, private dining room in the restaurant which they patronized so frequently when Mason was in court.

Mason, regarding his plate in frowning concentration, hardly touched his food. "They've got everything mixed up now," he said at length.

"You mean the ice pick?" Drake asked.

Mason nodded. "Their anxiety to force an identification of the defendant as the one who purchased the murder weapon means they got the wrong person, and if they did that, they must have the wrong ice pick."

"After all," Della Street said, "there is a certain superficial resemblance between Mildred Crest and me."

Mason nodded. "This is just another one of those cases of mistaken personal identification.

"In the mind of the average man, circumstantial evidence most frequently results in a miscarriage of justice. Actually, circumstantial evidence is the best evidence we have. It is only our interpretation of circumstantial evidence which makes for miscarriages of justice. The most deadly, dangerous evidence, the one which has resulted so many, many times in miscarriages of justice, is personal identification evidence."

"But how do you know they have the wrong ice pick?" Drake asked.

Mason said, "I planted one ice pick in Harrod's apartment at a time when I was satisfied he was trying to lay a foundation for blackmail. I hoped Harrod might become confused. Of course, at the time I had no idea he was fatally wounded."

"And now you think it was Nellie who became confused?" Drake asked.

"Not Nellie," Mason said. "The police were the ones who walked into the trap."

"What happened?"

"They found that some woman, whom they may or may not know was Katherine Baylor, had bought three ice picks; that thereafter some other woman had been in and bought three more, and that this second purchase could be differentiated from the first because there was a different price tag."

"So what happened?" Della Street asked.

"They talked to the girl who was running the place. She remembered the two transactions. Naturally, it occurred to the police that if they could prove that Mildred Crest was the one who bought the second batch of ice picks, and that those ice picks could be distinguished by the new price mark, they would have a perfect case against Mildred."

"And so they forced an identification?" Paul Drake asked.

"They probably forced the identification to this extent— they arranged for Irma Karnes to have an opportunity to see Mildred Crest when Mildred didn't know she was under observation. They didn't have a line-up. They simply gave the witness an opportunity for a surreptitious survey.

"And, of course, they used all their power of suggestion in telling Irma Karnes that they knew they had the girl in custody who had bought the ice picks; that it was simply a question of having her make the identification."

"So she made the identification?" Della Street asked.

Mason nodded.

"Just watch the expression on the face of that witness when she sees me!" Della said gleefully.

"Just how are you going to spring your trap?" Drake asked Mason.

"There," Mason said, "is the question. This is a case of mistaken identification. It's like any one of a thousand other cases. Only in this case we know the answer. *We* know the real purchaser and the police don't. When I confront this witness with Della Street, and the witness recognizes Della as the one who made the subsequent purchase of ice picks, there'll be a lot of commotion in court."

"But suppose she doesn't remember it was Della?" Drake asked.

"Then," Mason said thoughtfully, "my client might be in one hell of a jam, Paul. Of course, Della can always get on the stand and swear that she was the one who bought the ice picks, but in view of the fact she is working with me, her testimony would be taken with a grain of salt. . . . Judge Bolton will believe her, I think."

"The judge would," Drake said, "but how about a jury later on?"

"There, of course, is the rub," Mason admitted. "Judge Bolton knows me well enough to know that, if I put Della Street on the stand, it will be because I am absolutely convinced of the truth of her testimony. He doesn't know Della Street personally, but he knows she has been with me for a long while and is a trusted, confidential employee. He'll believe her.

"However, when Irma Karnes sees Della Street, it's almost certain that she will then realize she has made a mistake and will change her testimony."

"So what do you do?" Drake asked.

"So," Mason said, "I cross-examine this woman. I tie her up and get her so far out on a limb that when she is forced to back up she goes all to pieces."

"Then what happens?" Drake asked.

"Then," Mason said, "even if Judge Bolton binds the defendant over, I have a record on this witness so that when I get her in front of a jury later on, I'll mix her up like scrambled eggs. She'll be giving her entire testimony on the defensive."

"How about waiting until you do get her in front of a jury?" Drake asked. "Wouldn't it be better, since Judge Bolton will probably bind the defendant over anyway, to wait and pull this in front of a jury?"

"It would be better in many ways," Mason said, "but there's one thing against it."

"What?"

"The longer interval of time that elapses, the less likelihood there is that she'll change her testimony. By the time the case comes to trial in the superior court, she might even be so firmly convinced of her identification that she'll swear it was the defendant and that she had never seen Della Street in her life.

"No, I'm going to have to do it now in order to get the most good out of it. Even if she doesn't back up, the prosecutor will know that I wouldn't make a move of that sort unless it was true. They'll start hammering away at her between now and the time Mildred Crest goes to trial in the superior court. Then, by the time Irma Karnes gets on the stand in front of a jury, her entire attitude will be that of a woman who is very much on the defensive.

"However, the big thing is that, because of this fluke of identification, they *must have the wrong murder weapon.* Once the case gets to that point, there are infinite possibilities."

Drake said, "I'm going to be holding onto my chair watching what happens this afternoon."

"What do you want me to do?" Della Street asked.

"Keep out of sight," Mason said. "Irma Karnes probably saw you this morning, but I don't want her to see you any more until I call you to confront her. You can stay in one of the witness rooms and be available when I call you.

"When I do, that will show that you were the one who bought the new ice picks and then we've got the case on ice."

"But what will they say about the ethics of putting that ice pick in Harrod's apartment?"

"What *can* they say?" Mason asked. "We simply took an ice pick up to Harrod's apartment so I could ask Harrod if the ice pick with which he had been stabbed was identical to the one we had. Inadvertently, that ice pick was left in Harrod's apartment."

"But I can't swear to that," Della Street said.

"Bless your soul!" Mason told her. "*We* don't swear to anything except the truth. Your testimony is simply going to be that you bought three ice picks; that you took one of them up to Harrod's apartment, and that you left it there; that you were acting under my instructions."

"Will *you* then get on the stand?" Della Street asked apprehensively.

Mason shook his head. "I'll say to the Court that it's up to the prosecution to prove every step of its case. Everyone will know that I set a trap for Carl Harrod, and that the police walked into it. My justification will be that at the time I set the trap I thought I was dealing with a civil suit for damages. I had no idea of confusing the evidence in a murder case. . . . The main point is that the prosecution's entire case will turn out to be founded on incorrect evidence, an erroneous identification of the defendant, and the wrong ice pick as a murder weapon. That will leave the police and the deputy district attorney with very red faces."

"Well," Drake said, "it sounds all right the way you tell it, but somehow I have an idea that you're going to be walking on a tightrope over a very deep precipice."

Mason merely nodded.

"Well," Drake said, "you'd better be getting on up there. Then we'll see what's going to happen."

"On our way," Mason told him, glancing at his wrist watch. "This is where I'm going to have to ask just exactly the right questions in just exactly the right way. It's also a darned good lesson in the value of personal identification testimony. Here we have a case that's brought right home to us. And the worst of it is, Della, that mistaken identification could just as well have involved you in a murder if the circumstances had been different."

"How do you know it's not going to involve her in a murder the way it is?" Drake asked quietly.

Mason thought that over, then said, "Come on, Della. Let's go before Paul talks you into being guilty of killing Harrod."

"I wish I could sit in court this afternoon," Della Street ventured.

"Absolutely not," Mason told her firmly.

"Not even if I sat in the back row?"

"No, you might spring the trap too soon. I've got to play this *exactly* right."

"You can say *that* again," Paul Drake announced lugubriously.

"And in the meantime, Paul," Mason said, "I want to know where Fern Driscoll's car is."

"Why?"

"Because I want to search it for evidence. Call your office and start your bloodhounds baying."

"Okay," Drake said. "We'll get busy."

13

JUDGE BOLTON SAID, "Let the record show the defendant is in court; that counsel for both sides are in attendance. I believe the witness, Irma Karnes, was on the stand and the direct examination had been concluded. Cross-examination on behalf of the defense was about to begin.

"Take the stand, Miss Karnes."

Irma Karnes walked to the stand with her long-legged stiff-backed gait and looked at Perry Mason, blinking her eyes behind the thick-lensed glasses.

Mason said affably and casually, "I take it you wear those glasses all the time, Miss Karnes?"

"No, sir," she said.

"No?" Mason asked.

"No."

"When can you dispense with them?"

"When I'm asleep."

Laughter rippled through the courtroom. Irma Karnes held her face completely without expression so that it was impossible to tell whether she had deliberately set the stage for her remark or whether she was a literal-minded person who carefully took every statement at its face value.

"Do you," Mason asked, "know who the first young woman was who purchased three of the ice picks?"

"I do now. I didn't then."

"You know now?"

"Yes."

"Who was it?"

"Miss Katherine Baylor."

"And when did you learn that it was Miss Katherine Baylor?"

Calvert said, "Just a moment. Your Honor, I object on the ground that this is not proper cross-examination; that it is incompetent, irrelevant and immaterial."

Judge Bolton shook his head. "The witness mentioned the first purchase. In fact, the witness made it an important part of her testimony. Therefore, counsel is entitled to go into it. Answer the question."

"It was . . . I don't know, rather recently."

"Who told you it was Katherine Baylor?"

"The police."

"The police told you Katherine Baylor was the young woman who purchased those first three ice picks?"

"Yes."

"Then the only knowledge that you have on this point is what the police told you?"

"No, sir. That's not right."

"Well, what *is* right?"

"They told me who it was, but they said they wanted me to take a look at her so I could be sure."

"In other words, *they gave you* the information, and then told you they wanted you to look so *you* could make an identification?"

"Well, yes."

"You knew you were expected to make the identification before you saw Miss Baylor?"

"Oh, Your Honor," Calvert said, "this is consuming the time of the Court and making a mountain out of a molehill. If counsel is at all concerned about the matter, *I'll* state that Katherine Baylor not only doesn't deny purchasing those first three ice picks, but presently I'm going to put her on the witness stand and she's going to testify to it."

"The fact remains, if the Court please," Mason said, "I am entitled to cross-examine this witness in my own way."

Judge Bolton nodded. "I think I see the point counsel is leading up to. Go right ahead."

"Isn't that a fact?" Mason asked the witness. "You knew that you were expected to make an identification of Miss Baylor as soon as you saw her?"

"I don't know what the police expected. I'm not a mind reader."

Mason said, "I'm not asking you what the police expected you to do. I'm asking you whether you knew what you were expected to do."

"I can't say."

"They told you that you were going to see Miss Baylor?"

"Yes."

"And they told you that she was the young woman who had made the first purchase of the three ice picks. Isn't that right?"

"Yes."

"So when you saw her, you knew that the police expected you to make the identification."

"Objected to as calling for a conclusion of the witness," Calvert said. "She can't testify as to what the police expected."

"The objection is sustained." Judge Bolton ruled.

"Well, the police *told* you that they expected you to make the identification, didn't they?"

"Not in so many words."

"At least by their actions and they also intimated that, didn't they?"

"Well, yes."

"Now then," Mason said, "when did you first know that it was Mildred Crest who made the second purchase of ice picks that night?"

"Just a short time after her arrest."

"What do you mean by the expression, a short time?"

"I mean it was only a short time."

"Two or three days?"

"Sooner."

"And did the police follow the same procedure in that instance? Did *they* tell *you* that Mildred Crest was the person who had purchased the second lot of three ice picks?"

"It was my understanding that she had."

"And did they tell you they expected you to make an identification?"

"Well, I knew that the police were certain she had made the purchase. Then when I saw her, *I* knew that she was the one who had made the purchase."

"You identified her to the police?"

"Yes."

"Did you meet her face to face?"

"I saw her clearly."

"Did you talk with her?"

"No."

"Did you hear her voice?"

"Yes."

"Where did this identification take place?"

"It was in a room—an interrogation room. There's a big mirror at one end of the room. That is, it's a mirror which shows a reflection to any person on the inside

130

looking out, but it's a window to anyone who is in the adjoining room looking in. You see very distinctly, but the person in the other room can't see you at all."

"So you sat in this observation room and the defendant was ushered into the interrogation room and you looked at her through the one-way mirror, did you not?"

"Yes."

"And was there an officer with you at that time?"

"Yes."

"More than one?"

"Yes."

"How many?"

"Three."

"And did those officers make comments?"

"They were talking."

"To you?"

"Yes, and among themselves."

"And the gist of their conversation was that the defendant, Mildred Crest, was the girl who had purchased the ice picks, isn't that true?"

"They mentioned something to that effect. They were also discussing other things."

"Things which were calculated to prejudice you against the defendant, discussing the fact that she was supposed to have murdered Fern Driscoll?"

"They said something like that."

"Just what did they say?"

"I can't remember their exact words, but they said she had murdered Fern Driscoll, had stolen her money and, when Harrod found out about it, had stabbed him with an ice pick she bought from the store where I work."

"So *after* they said all that, you made the identification, did you?"

"Well, when I saw the defendant, I knew she was the one."

"Right away, the minute you saw her?"

"Yes."

"How long were you in the observation room?"

"About ten minutes, I guess."

"And how long were you in the observation room after the defendant was led into the interrogation room?"

"She was brought in within just a few seconds of the time I entered the observation room."

"And she was in the interrogation room all of the time you were in the observation room?"

"Yes."

"Which was a period of at least ten minutes?"

"I would say so."

"It could have been more?"

"Perhaps."

"But it couldn't have been less?"

"I think it was at least ten minutes."

"And during all of that time the officers were asking you to look the defendant over carefully?"

"Yes."

"Now then," Mason said, "if you made the identification as soon as the defendant walked in the room, what was the reason for the officers to keep you there for ten minutes, asking you to look the defendant over carefully?"

"Well, they said they wanted me to be sure."

"Weren't *you* sure?"

"I was, yes."

"You were sure when you left the room?"

"Yes."

"Were you sure before that?"

"I thought I was."

"Yet you kept looking at the defendant during all that ten-minute period?"

"Yes."

"Studying her features?"

"Yes."

"Why?"

"Well, the officers suggested— Am I at liberty to tell what they said?"

Calvert grinned. "Go right ahead. What *did* the officers say?"

"Well, they said that Mr. Mason was going to be representing the defendant, that he was noted for being tricky and that he might arrange to have some other young woman brought in and try to trick me that way. They said that I should study the defendant carefully so that Mr. Mason couldn't— Well, the way they expressed it was 'run in a ringer.' "

"And was that the reason you made such a careful study of the defendant?" Mason asked.

"Yes."

"For a period of ten minutes?"

"Yes."

"Now going back to the night of the second," Mason said, "what were your duties there at the Arcade Novelty Company?"

"Well, I acted as cashier."

"What were your duties as cashier?"

"To make change, giving out nickels, pennies and dimes as they were required."

"Anything else?"

"I sort of kept an eye on the various people to see what they were doing and see that everything was running in an orderly manner."

"Anything else?"

"No. That's about all."

"But you were also acting as saleslady?"

"Oh yes. I sold merchandise whenever anybody came in and wanted something."

"And wrapped the merchandise for them?"

"Usually I just dropped it in a paper bag."

"That took quite a bit of your time?"

"Not so much."

"Didn't quite a few people come in?"

"Well, it's a self-service place. That is, the people pick out what they want and bring it up to the cashier to be paid for and wrapped. About all I have to do is to ring up the money in the cash register and drop the articles in a paper bag. We keep an assortment of paper bags on a shelf right beneath the cash register."

"Then a big percentage of your time is put in making change for customers and watching what is going on in the Arcade?"

"Yes. Mostly watching, keeping an eye on things."

"You have quite a few customers?"

"Quite a few."

"And you try to keep an eye on what they're doing?"

"Yes. I have to make certain that things are run in an orderly manner; that the young men don't annoy the women who don't want to be annoyed."

"What do you mean by that?"

"Well, of course, if young women are sociably inclined and don't resent attention, why that's all right, but, if some young men become obnoxious or try to force their attentions on customers, then we do something about it."

"So you keep a sharp eye on what is going on?"

"Yes."

"I take it then that you're trained to see things that go on."

"Indeed I am, Mr. Mason. You have to have an eagle eye to run a place like that. You get so you're trained to see the faintest suspicion of a false motion."

"That is, you know what to look for?"

"Yes."

"And you keep looking?"

"Yes."

"Your spectacles have rather heavy correction?"

"I'm blind as a bat without my spectacles, but with them I see very well."

"Directly in front of you?"

"Yes."

"Your vision to the side is somewhat impaired?"

"Yes, but I can see all right. That's my job, to see what's going on."

"You're also making change at the cash register?" Mason asked.

"Yes. I said I was. I told you that."

"And ringing up purchases?"

"Yes."

"Suppose there would be a shortage at the cash register?"

"There never is. Not when I'm on duty."

"You don't make mistakes?"

"No."

"How does it happen you have such a perfect record?"

"Concentration largely."

"By that I take it you mean that, when you're making change, you think about making change and nothing else."

"Exactly."

"And you don't make mistakes?"

"I never have. My cash has always balanced out to the penny."

"When you're ringing up a sale," Mason said, "you concentrate on making the correct change?"

"Yes."

"And putting the proper amount of money in the proper compartment in the cash register?"

"Yes."

"During that time your eyes necessarily are averted from what is going on in the Arcade, are they not?"

"That is true, Mr. Mason. But you learn to make the interval as brief as possible. And even during that interval you're sort of keeping an eye on things with an occasional quick glance."

"I take it then," Mason said, "that even while you're smiling at the customer you're actually looking over past the customer's shoulder to see that the place is being operated in an orderly manner."

"That's right."

"Now, just how clearly do you remember the transaction when the person you say was the defendant bought the three ice picks?"

"Quite clearly."

"Do you remember whether she paid you the exact purchase price or—"

"Certainly I remember. She put down a five-dollar bill. I gave her her change and I remember telling her that the ice picks had been three for a dollar earlier in the evening, but that when I replenished the stock in the display case I noticed that the price had gone up and so put a new price tag on the ice picks."

"The ice picks were then forty-one cents straight?"

"That's right."

"So three ice picks amounted to a dollar and twenty-three cents?"

"Yes."

"Plus sales tax?"

"Yes."

"How long do you suppose the person you state was the defendant was standing in front of you? How long did the transaction take place?"

"Just a few seconds."

"You didn't have any extended conversation?"

"No."

"The customer just handed you the ice picks, you rang up the money, took out the change, dropped the ice picks in a bag and handed them to her with the comment that they had been cheaper earlier in the evening?"

"That is right, yes, sir."

"Did you do all that within a period of ten seconds, would you say?"

"Let me see. Ten seconds." The witness closed her eyes. "Yes. I think so. I would say that ten seconds would probably be just about the right time interval."

"Now, during that ten seconds," Mason said, "you were making change of a dollar and twenty-three cents, plus sales tax, out of a five-dollar bill?"

"Yes, sir."

"And during that time, following your custom, you were concentrating on the operation of the cash register, on putting the five-dollar bill in the proper receptacle, taking out the change and being sure that you had the right amount?"

"Yes, sir."

"And during a part of that time, while you were smiling at the customer, you were looking over her shoulder into the Arcade to make certain that everything was being conducted in an orderly manner?"

"I suppose so."

"That is your usual custom?"

"Yes."

"So that out of the ten-second interval you were actually looking at the person who you claim was the defendant for only a small portion of that time, perhaps two or three seconds?"

"Well . . . I saw her well enough to recognize her."

"Perhaps two or three seconds out of the ten-second interval you were looking directly at the customer?" Mason asked.

"Perhaps."

"Could it have been more?"

"Well, let's see. I was looking at the cash register and— Well, perhaps half of the time I was looking directly at the customer."

"That would be five seconds?"

"Yes."

"But while you were looking at her you were also looking over her shoulder past her at the Arcade?"

"I guess I did."

"So that would cut down the five seconds' time?"

"Yes."

"Yet," Mason said, "when you looked at the defendant at police headquarters so that you could be sure I didn't run a ringer in on you, *it took you ten minutes, ten full minutes,* during which you were concentrating *entirely* on the features of the defendant. It took you ten, long minutes before you could be sure that you wouldn't be led into a trap and that you'd know her when you saw her again?"

"Well . . . it wasn't necessary for me to look at her that long."

"Then why did you do it?"

"I wanted to be *absolutely* certain."

"It took you ten minutes before you were *absolutely* certain?"

"Oh, I suppose so, if you insist."

"Ten full minutes of concentrated study," Mason said, "as opposed to two and a half seconds' casual observation."

"Well, I— Of course, at the time of the purchase, I—"

"Exactly," Mason said. "At that time you didn't have any particular reason for studying the features of your customer. Whereas when you were looking at the defendant, you knew you were going to be called on to make an identification and you had to be absolutely positive that someone didn't trick you. Isn't that right?"

"Yes."

"Thank you," Mason said with a smile. "That's all."

Calvert hesitated as though debating whether to try and salvage something from the testimony concerning the time element, then apparently decided against it. "That's all," he said.

"Your next witness," Judge Bolton said.

"Call Katherine Baylor," Calvert said.

Katherine Baylor came to the stand, took the oath, gave her name and residence to the court reporter, looked to Calvert for questioning.

"You are acquainted with the defendant, Mildred Crest?"

"Yes."

"When did you first meet her?"

"On the second of this month."

"Where did you first meet her?"

"At her apartment."

"Under what name was she going when you met her?"

"Well, she admitted to me—"

"Kindly listen to the question," Calvert interrupted. "Under what name was she going when you first met her?"

"The name of Fern Driscoll."

"Did you, on the evening of the second, purchase some ice picks from the Arcade Novelty Company?"

"I did."

"How many ice picks?"

"Three."

"What did you pay for them?"

"One dollar."

"Do you remember the price that was marked on the ice picks?"

"Yes, sir. I do."

"What was the price?"

"It was thirty-eight cents, three for a dollar."

"What did you do with those ice picks?"

"I took them to the apartment with me."

"You mean the apartment that the defendant was occupying under the name of Fern Driscoll?"

"Yes."

"And what did you do with them there?"

"I put one of them in my purse, and left the other two there on a table by the entranceway."

"And did you have some conversation with the defendant about them?"

"Yes."

"About using them?"

"Yes."

"About using them in what way?"

"As weapons."

"What did you tell her?"

"I told her an ice pick made a wonderful weapon; that if you needed to make a man keep his distance, an ice pick would do the trick."

"Did you say anything else about them?"

"I suggested putting a cork on the end of the ice pick so that it could be carried in a purse."

"And you put one of those ice picks in your purse?"

"Yes."

"Now, Miss Baylor, you are under oath. I want you to think carefully. Did you have any conversation with the defendant in which she told you she wanted these ice picks as weapons to use against Carl Harrod?"

"No."

"She didn't tell you that?"

"No."

"Or words to that effect?"

"No."

"You gave her these ice picks as weapons?"

"Yes."

"Did *you* suggest she use them, or one of them, as a weapon to intimidate Carl Harrod?"

The witness hesitated.

"Did you?"

"I told her if Carl Harrod tried any more blackmail, she could threaten him with an ice pick—to protect herself—in self-defense."

"And she accepted these ice picks from you after that conversation?"

"I just left them there in her apartment."

"Thank you. That's all. The defense may take the witness."

"Did you ever meet Carl Harrod in his lifetime?" Mason asked.

"I met him, yes."

"How did you happen to meet him?"

"He came to the defendant's apartment while I was there."

"What did you do?"

"I opened the door."

"He was standing there?"

"He was standing there."

"You recognized him?"

"He told me who he was."

"And what did you do?"

"I told him how I felt about blackmailers and then slapped his face."

"Did you, at that time, stab him with an ice pick?"

"Certainly not!"

"You say that you put one of these ice picks in your purse?"

"Yes."

"Why?"

"Because I wanted to carry it with me."

"Why?"

"To protect myself."

"Against whom?"

"Against anyone who might attack me."

"Did you feel that someone might attack you?"

"Yes."

"Who?"

"I have told you, Mr. Mason, I had slapped Carl Harrod's face. I was under no illusions about the character of Carl Harrod. He was a blackmailer who had—"

"Now, just a moment! Just a moment!" Calvert interrupted. "If the Court please, I feel that the witness should be admonished only to answer questions, not to volunteer any disparaging remarks concerning the character of the deceased."

Judge Bolton said, "I think, Mr. Prosecutor, the situation is obvious. The Court was not born yesterday. However, the law is the law, and the character of a decedent in a murder case is not in issue. However, the witness will refrain from making statements as to the character of the decedent."

"You felt you might have some trouble with Carl Harrod?" Mason asked.

"Yes."

"And for that reason put an ice pick in your purse?"

"Yes."

"Where is that ice pick now?"

"I don't know."

"You don't know?"

"No."

"Where was it when you saw it last?"

"I . . . I threw it away."

"And why did you do that?"

"Someone suggested that I should."

"Your father?"

"Yes."

"And why did your father make that suggestion?"

"We knew that Carl Harrod had been stabbed with an ice pick. My father knew that I had slapped his face. I told him about buying the ice picks. He suggested I had better get rid of the one that I had."

"When did this conversation take place?"

"On the second of this month, the day Harrod died."

"Do you remember that I visited your father on that date?"

"Yes."

"And while I was there, Sgt. Holcomb telephoned?"

"I believe so. Yes."

"Now then, when did you dispose of the ice pick with reference to my visit?"

"Immediately after you left and before Sgt. Holcomb came."

"And what did you do with it?"

"I took the elevator to the freight entrance. I went out in the alley where there were some trash cans. I raised the lid of one of the trash cans, put the ice pick in there, and then returned to the room."

"You were back in your suite at the hotel before Sgt. Holcomb arrived?"

"Yes."

"Did you tell him about what you had done with the ice pick?"

"No."

"Did you tell anyone?"

"No. I refused to discuss my testimony with anyone. I said that I would tell my story on the witness stand and that I wouldn't talk before I got on the witness stand."

"I see," Mason said. "You did, however, admit buying the three ice picks?"

"My father did, after Sgt. Holcomb told him that Carl Harrod had told his wife I had slapped his face, and that—"

"Just a moment," Calvert interrupted. "I object to the witness relating any conversation which took place with Sgt. Holcomb. That is hearsay."

"On the contrary, Your Honor," Mason said. "It is a fact in this case, so far as it concerns the motivation or bias of this witness. I am entitled to show the attitude of mind of this witness insofar as it may pertain to any bias either for or against the defense."

"The objection is overruled," Judge Bolton said. "Go on with your statement, Miss Baylor."

"Well, Sgt. Holcomb said that Mrs. Harrod, or the woman who was supposed to be Mrs. Harrod, had told the police that I had slapped Carl Harrod's face, and that, when Mr. Mason had been there getting a statement from Mr. Harrod, he had insinuated I was the one who had stabbed Harrod with an ice pick. Under the circumstances, Sgt. Holcomb suggested that a determined attempt might be made to have it appear I had done the stabbing and . . . and he didn't want to have that happen."

"Did you tell him about buying the ice picks?"

"No, *I* didn't tell him. My father told him. I made no statement whatever. I simply sat there."

"And Sgt. Holcomb didn't question you?"

"No."

"But talked with your father?"

"Yes."

Mason smiled. "Did Sgt. Holcomb say to your father that it might be better if he didn't question you at all until after he knew more of the facts, so that you wouldn't be a vulnerable witness in case I should take you on cross-examination?"

"Something like that."

"And your father told Sgt. Holcomb that you had purchased the three ice picks and given them to the defendant?"

"Yes."

"And did Sgt. Holcomb ask you or your father what had happened to the missing ice pick?"

"No, sir," she said. "He didn't know one was missing. They were all there in the apartment. That was the thing I couldn't understand; but I said nothing and my father said nothing. I don't think the officers knew about any other ice pick."

"Now then," Mason said, "you gave the defendant two of the ice picks?"

"Yes."

"To be used as weapons in case of necessity?"

"Yes."

"Can you suggest any reason why the defendant, having two ice picks which you had given her to be used as weapons, should go down to the Arcade Novelty Company and buy three more ice picks?"

"No, sir, I cannot. I have discussed that matter with my father, and we decided—"

"Just a moment!" Calvert interrupted. "We object to any statement as to what she said to her father or what her father said to her."

"The objection is sustained," Judge Bolton said. "In fact, the entire question asked by the defense counsel is argumentative."

"I have no objection to the question on that ground," Calvert said. "The prosecution has its own theory in the matter, and I think it is obvious. If Mr. Mason cross-examines this witness as to the reason the defendant might have had for purchasing those three ice picks, I intend to go into the matter on redirect examination."

"That's the vice of these questions which go far afield," Judge Bolton said. "The Court will of its own motion terminate this line of cross-examination. That question is argumentative, and the witness need not answer."

"The prosecution feels it is obvious, Your Honor," Calvert said, "that the defendant in this case wanted the crime blamed on Katherine Baylor. Knowing that Katherine Baylor had taken *one* of the ice picks away in her purse, the defendant purchased other ice picks so that the police would be led to believe that the two ice picks Katherine Baylor had given the defendant were still in the defendant's apartment, and therefore couldn't have been used in inflicting the fatal stabbing. This, if the Court please, is one of the strongest points in our case, because it shows premeditation. If it hadn't been for the peculiar quirk of fate by which there were different price tags on the ice picks, the defendant's ruse might have gone undetected."

"You can argue the case after the evidence is in," Judge Bolton said. "As far as this witness is concerned, I don't care to have her interrogated as to the possible motives of the defendant. I suggest, however, that it is significant that this witness disposed of the ice pick she had in the manner she did."

Calvert shrugged his shoulders. "Of course, Your Honor, the witness was acting under the advice of her father, and her father knew that Mr. Perry Mason— Well, he knew his reputation and knew that Mr. Mason would confuse the issues if it was at all possible."

"They're confused now," Mason said.

"Not to the prosecution, they aren't," Calvert snapped.

"That will do," Judge Bolton ruled. "Are there any further questions of this witness?"

"None, Your Honor," Mason said.

"Your next witness?" Judge Bolton asked Calvert.

"My next witness," Calvert announced, "is Nellie Elliston."

The woman Mason had seen in Harrod's apartment came forward. She was dressed in a neat, new outfit, well shod, with lustrous, sheer stockings, and had evidently spent some time in a beauty shop.

After she had given her name and address, Calvert started questioning her and in questioning pulled no punches.

"Your name is Nellie Elliston?"

"Yes."

"Have you ever gone under any other name?"

"Yes."

"What?"

"Mrs. Carl Harrod."

"Were you married to Harrod?"

"No."

"You were, however, living with him as his wife?"

"Yes."

"In Apartment 218 at the Dixiecrat Apartments?"

"That's right."

"How long had you known Harrod?"

"About two years."

"Where did you meet him?"

"In a bar."

"How soon did you commence living with him after you first met him?"

"About a week."

"You assumed the name of Nellie Harrod purely as a matter of convenience?"

"Yes."

"Calling your attention to the second of this month, you were then living with Carl Harrod at the Dixiecrat Apartments as his wife?"

"I was using his name. We were going to be married. There were some legal complications. We didn't wait for those to be ironed out."

"Well," Calvert said, his voice radiating approval, "thank you for being so frank, Miss Elliston, even at the expense of your good name and reputation. I am sure the Court will appreciate it. Now, can you tell us exactly what happened on the night of the second?"

"Carl had been out. He came back about— Oh, I don't know, about eight-thirty or nine o'clock. He had had a nosebleed. He got some fresh handkerchiefs and changed his shirt. I asked him what had happened and he said a girl had smashed him; that she had taken him entirely by surprise."

"Then what?"

"I asked him what he did to her and he said nothing; that she had slammed the door before he had a chance."

"And then what?"

"Then he went out again. I had an idea he was going back—"

"Never mind your ideas," Calvert interrupted. "Just answer questions and give us the facts. The Court isn't interested in what you may have thought, only in the facts."

"Yes, sir."

"Now, he went out and then what happened? When did you see him again?"

"He came back in about— Oh, I don't know, about something over an hour, perhaps an hour and a half. I didn't check the time."

"And what was his condition at that time?"

"He was coughing. He coughed up a speck or two of blood. At first I thought it was from the—"

"Tut, tut," Calvert chided, holding up his finger and smiling. "Not your thoughts, Miss Elliston, just what you know."

"Yes, he came back and told me—"

"Now, just a moment. At that time, did he say anything to you about the fact that he thought he might be going to die?"

"No."

"Do you know from anything he said whether he thought any injury he might have had at that time was fatal?"

"He didn't think it was fatal. He was thinking only in terms of collecting damages. He actually was jubilant. He said we'd have some real money coming in and that then he could get the legal difficulties straightened out and then we could be married and go abroad on a honeymoon."

"Very well. Then I don't think it is proper for you to tell the Court anything he may have said at *that* time. You can tell us what happened and that's all."

"Well, he telephoned the Drake Detective Agency and said he wanted to get in touch with Mr. Perry Mason. Then when he got Perry Mason on the telephone he told him—"

"Now, there again, I doubt if that is pertinent," Calvert said. "And, of course, you don't know of your own knowledge that he had Mr. Mason on the other end of the telephone, do you? You simply heard one end of the conversation?"

"Yes."

"So you can't testify that Mr. Mason was on the other end of the line. After that, what happened?"

"Then Mr. Mason came and his secretary, Miss Della Street, was with him."

"And what happened at that time?"

"Well, Carl told Mr. Mason that he had been stabbed—"

"Now, just a minute. Did he expect to die at that time? That is, did he believe death was imminent because of some wound he had received?"

"No, sir, he did not. He was still trying to lay the foundation for collecting big damages."

"Then I feel that is not a proper statement. In other words, it was not a dying declaration within the meaning of the law. Just go ahead and tell us what happened. Did Mr. Mason and Miss Street leave?"

"They left."

"And then what happened?"

"Carl had been putting on an act to impress Mr. Mason. He said he was having a chill. At least, I thought it was an act, and—"

"Not your thoughts, *please*," Calvert interrupted. "We want the facts—only the facts."

"Well, after Mr. Mason left, he said he was cold and I suggested a hot bath. I drew the bath and told him it was ready.

"Then Carl started to get up out of the chair and then all of a sudden he began to feel worse. He almost collapsed. His face became pale as ashes and a look of the most horrible surprise came over his face and he said, 'Nellie, Nellie, I'm dying!' "

"Then at *that* time did he go on and make any statement to you as to what had happened at the time he had received the wound or injury?"

"Yes, sir."

"Now then, I believe that is a dying declaration within the meaning of the law. I believe that you are entitled to relate what he said; just tell us what he said had happened."

Judge Bolton looked down at Perry Mason. "Any objection from the defense?"

"No objection," Mason said, "but I would like to examine the witness for the purpose of laying the foundation as to a dying declaration."

"Proceed," Judge Bolton said.

"He told you he was going to die?" Mason asked.

"At that time, yes."

"And how long was that before he died?"

"Only a few minutes. I don't believe it was over ten minutes."

"There had then been a sudden change in his condition from the time I saw him?"

"Yes. It started when he tried to get up. He got partway up and then fell back. It was then that look of horrible consternation, surprise, and I think a little of terror, came over his face."

"He said he was dying?"

"He said, 'Nellie, that damned wound is— Something's happened. It's reached my heart, I guess. I'm . . . I'm dying.' "

"And then what?"

"Then he clutched his chest and said, 'Nellie, I don't want to die.' "

"And then what happened?"

"Then is when he made the statement."

Mason nodded to Calvert. "It would seem to be a dying declaration within the meaning of the law. I have no objection. Let her go ahead and tell what happened."

"Very well," Calvert said. "I am satisfied that it is a dying declaration. Just go ahead, Miss Elliston, and tell what happened. At this time you may relate what he said; use his exact words if you can remember them. If you can't, give your best recollection of what he said."

"He said that he had gone back to the defendant's apartment, that he had decided to show her who was boss, that if she would give him the letters she had, he wouldn't expose her.

"He said that she was using Fern Driscoll's name but she was really Mildred Crest. He said she had murdered Fern Driscoll and he felt he could prove it."

"Did he say anything about accusing her of murder?"

"Yes. He said that she came to the door; that she finally let him in; that he made his proposition to her."

"Then what?" Calvert asked.

"He said she laughed at him, that she told him he was a blackmailer, that she felt he had a police record, that if he didn't get out and stay out, she would claim she had found him burglarizing her apartment and shoot him.

"He said they had words and that she was holding the door open for him, telling him to get out. He said that suddenly, just as he was leaving, she swung her fist against his chest, then slammed and locked the door.

"He said that he didn't realize she had had an ice pick in her hand until he was almost to the elevator, that then he saw the ice pick sticking in his chest.

"He said that he didn't think he was badly hurt, but he felt he could use the girl's action as a lever to make her lawyer, Perry Mason, turn over the letters to him, that he could then get a large sum of money, either from the magazine, or from Mr. Baylor."

"What happened to the ice pick?"

"He brought it home with him."

"He told you that the pick he brought home was the one with which he had been stabbed?"

"Yes."

"Where is that ice pick now?"

"I gave it to the police."

"Did you mark that ice pick in some way so that you would know it again if you saw it?"

"Yes."

"What did you do?"

"I scratched my initials on the wooden handle."

"When?"

"Before it left the apartment."

"I now show you an ice pick and ask you if that is the ice pick you have been referring to?"

"That is the one."

"I will show that to counsel for the defense," Calvert said, "and then ask that it be introduced in evidence."

Calvert stepped over to the counsel table and handed the ice pick to Mason.

Mason studied the ice pick carefully. "May I ask a few questions on the exhibit, Your Honor?"

"Certainly," Judge Bolton said.

Mason turned to the witness. "I notice that this ice pick has a price mark on it, a price tag which is placed on with some sort of adhesive and covered with a piece of transparent tape. This price tag bears the label of the Arcade Novelty Company and the mark 'forty-one cents.' Was this price tag on the ice pick when you received it from Carl Harrod?"

"Yes."

"You are *positive* this is the ice pick that Carl Harrod gave you?"

"Yes."

"This is the ice pick Carl Harrod told you had been pushed into his chest?"

"Yes."

"He handed you this ice pick?"

"Yes."

"And you marked it?"

"Yes."

"When did you mark it?"

"When the police came."

"One of the officers suggested that you should mark this ice pick?"

"Yes, sir."

"So that you wouldn't be confused when it came time to give your testimony?"

"So that it could be identified."

"Were there any other ice picks in your apartment?"

"Yes, there was one other."

"Where?"

"In the kitchen drawer."

"By that you mean a utility drawer in the kitchen?"

"Yes."

"What else did that drawer contain?"

"Some cooking spoons, a bottle opener, a few little things of that sort."

"Very good," Mason said. "Now, I'm anxious to get this straight: were there *two* ice picks in this utility drawer?"

"Yes."

"Do you mean that you put the ice pick with which Carl Harrod had been stabbed in the utility drawer?"

"Yes."

"How did that happen? Didn't you realize that—?"

"Carl came home. He seemed to be high."

"What do you mean by being high?"

"I mean high! You know the way a person is when he's high."

"He'd been drinking?"

"No."

"Marijuana?"

"Yes."

"And what did he say?"

"He seemed very jubilant. He told me that he'd really hit the jackpot."

"And then what?"

"He told me that he was a good provider. He said he'd

bought me an ice pick, and he tossed that ice pick in the sink."

"And then?"

"I asked him what on earth we wanted an ice pick for. I told him we used ice cubes and had no need for an ice pick."

"And then?"

"Then he went in the other room, sat down, and we talked for a while. Then I went back to the kitchen. I noticed there was a little pinkish stain in the sink where the point of the ice pick had rested in a drop of water, but I thought nothing of it. I picked the ice pick up, washed it, and put it in the drawer."

"You *washed* it?"

"Yes, I *washed* it!"

"Why?"

"I didn't know where Carl had secured it or anything, and he'd been carrying it around with him. I always wash dishes and utensils before putting them away."

"Did you at that time know there was an ice pick in the drawer?"

"Very frankly, Mr. Mason, I didn't. It came as a great surprise to me after the police had asked me to produce the ice pick, when I opened the kitchen drawer and found that there were two of them."

"Is there any chance— Now I want you to listen to this very carefully," Mason said, "and I want you to consider your answer very carefully—is there *any* chance, any *possible* chance that you got the ice picks confused?"

"Absolutely not!"

"How do you know you didn't?"

"Because the ice pick that I put in that drawer was put in at a certain place, right near the front of the drawer, and this second ice pick was way in the back of the drawer. Moreover, there was no price tag on the other ice pick. I remember distinctly that the ice pick Carl brought home with him had this price tag on it."

"You're positive?"

"I'm absolutely positive."

Mason nodded to the prosecutor. "Under the circumstances, I have no further questions and no objection to the ice pick being received in evidence."

"The ice pick will be received," Judge Bolton said.

"That concludes my direct examination of the witness, Your Honor," Calvert said.

"Cross-examine," Judge Bolton said to Perry Mason.

Mason regarded the witness thoughtfully for a moment, then said, "While I was talking with Carl Harrod, didn't he admit that the light was dim and he couldn't be certain that it was the defendant who had stabbed him? Didn't he admit there was a possibility that Katherine Baylor had opened the door and stabbed him?"

"Just a moment! Just a moment!" Calvert shouted. "Don't answer that question, Miss Elliston. Now then, Your Honor, I wish to interpose an objection on the ground that this is incompetent, irrelevant, and immaterial, that it is not proper cross-examination.

"It appears now conclusively that, at the time Mr. Mason was talking with Carl Harrod, Carl Harrod was only putting on an act. He was trying to collect damages. He had no idea that he was about to die. The whole theory of the law under which dying declarations are permitted to be received in evidence is that the law presumes that a person who is about to die, knowing that nothing he can say or do will give him any material advantage, having been brought face to face with a situation where only spiritual assets can count, is going to tell the truth, at least to the same extent that he would if he were testifying under oath on the witness stand."

"I understand the theory of the law in regard to dying declarations," Judge Bolton said drily. "I think you may rest assured that the Court understands the elemental principles of law."

"Yes, Your Honor, I merely commented on it in order

to show that there is a great difference between a true, dying declaration which is made when a person thinks he is going to die, and a spurious dying declaration which is a part of a fraudulent scheme by which a person is trying to get damages."

"I understand all that," Judge Bolton said, "but let us suppose that a dying declaration is given the force of testimony under oath. If Carl Harrod had testified under oath, Mr. Mason would have been permitted to ask him if he hadn't made some different statement at a different time, wouldn't he?"

"Certainly, Your Honor, but that's a different situation. Mr. Mason would then be asking Carl Harrod himself, and Carl Harrod would have the opportunity to explain any seeming inconsistencies. Now he is asking a third party about some so-called contradictory statement made by Harrod. It seems to me we are getting into the realm of hearsay."

"Nevertheless," Judge Bolton said, "I am interested in hearing the answer of the witness. I'd like to have the question answered. The objection is overruled."

"Very well," Calvert said, yielding with poor grace.

Judge Bolton turned to the witness. "Did he make some such statement, Miss Elliston?"

"I don't think so, Your Honor. I know that Mr. Mason was trying to mix him up and—"

"Now, never mind what you think Mr. Mason was trying to do," Judge Bolton said sternly. "I want to know what Carl Harrod said."

"Well, Mr. Mason brought out the fact that the light was rather poor, and then asked Carl how he could be certain it hadn't been Katherine Baylor who had stabbed him."

"And what did Mr. Harrod say?"

"Well, he became indignant and said he didn't intend to have Mr. Mason cross-examine him."

"Very well," Judge Bolton said to Mason. "Continue with your cross-examination, Counselor."

"Did Carl Harrod telephone Mr. Baylor after I left and in connection with the suggestion I had made?"

"He—"

"Just a minute!" Calvert interrupted. "Refrain from answering, if you will, until I have an opportunity to put in an objection. . . . If the Court please, I object to that question on the ground that it is incompetent, irrelevant, and immaterial, that it calls for hearsay evidence, that it calls for a conclusion of the witness, that it assumes a fact not in evidence, and that it is not proper cross-examination. I didn't go into any of these matters on direct examination. My direct examination was confined to the dying declaration with sufficient factual background of what had gone before to explain the situation."

"Well, let's consider this as part of the factual background," Judge Bolton said.

"Moreover, Your Honor, it calls for a conclusion of the witness, and it's argumentative. She doesn't know who was on the other end of the line."

"Do you know whether Carl Harrod called up Mr. Harriman Baylor after Mr. Mason left?" Judge Bolton asked the witness.

"No, sir."

"You don't know?"

"No, sir."

"Continue with your cross-examination, Mr. Mason," Judge Bolton said.

"Did he call up someone?"

"He used the telephone. Yes."

"Did you see the number he dialed?"

"No."

"Did you hear the person he asked for?"

She hesitated a moment, then said, "No."

"Did you hear him call the other party by name over

the telephone? Did you hear him address that party as Mr. Baylor?"

"Just a moment! Just a moment!" Calvert said. "If the Court please, that is objected to on the ground that it isn't binding on the prosecution if a witness addresses someone by name over the telephone. I might call up Your Honor and say, 'Now listen, Mr. President . . .' and that wouldn't mean I was talking to the President of the United States."

"I understand," Judge Bolton said, "but that objection goes to the weight rather than to the admissibility of the evidence. I feel all this is part of the *res gestae*. I think I'll hear the answer. Did he telephone someone whom he addressed as Mr. Baylor?"

"Yes, he did."

"Thank you," Mason said smiling. "That's all!"

"Just a moment," Calvert said. "I have some redirect examination. You heard him use the name Baylor. You don't know whether he was talking with Mr. Baylor or Miss Baylor, do you?"

"I think he said, 'Mister.' "

"All right, then you don't *know* whether he was talking with Harriman Baylor or with Forrester Baylor, his son?"

"No, sir, that I don't know."

"And you don't even know whether the person he was addressing wasn't some stranger by the name of Baylor, some other Baylor altogether?"

"That's right. I don't."

"And you didn't hear him use the person's first name?"

"You mean at that conversation that took place after Mr. Mason left?"

"Yes."

"No, I didn't hear him use any given name."

"That's all," Calvert said.

"Just a minute," Mason said. "You referred specifically to the conversation he had after I left. Do you mean there were two conversations?"

"Yes, sir."

"When did the first conversation take place?"

"Very shortly after my husband returned to the apartment."

"And whom did he call then?"

"I don't know."

"Whom did he ask for?"

"He asked for Mr. Baylor."

"But you heard him call the person at the other end of the line 'Baylor' on both occasions?"

"Yes."

"He used the words 'Mr. Baylor?' "

"Yes."

"Then, as I understand it, he made one call immediately after returning home, and before you knew he had been stabbed with an ice pick, and the second call at a later time after I left. Is that right?"

"Yes."

"Thank you," Mason said, "I think that's all.

"However, in view of this testimony I do have one further question on cross-examination of the witness Irma Karnes."

"I object to having counsel conduct his cross-examination piecemeal," Calvert said. "He had an opportunity to cross-examine Miss Karnes, and he should have concluded his cross-examination. I don't think it is fair to the prosecution to have witnesses called back for further cross-examination from time to time."

"The conduct of the examination is entirely in the discretion of the Court," Judge Bolton said. "It appears to the Court, in view of the circumstances surrounding the testimony of this last witness, that we should attempt to get at the truth of the case."

Judge Bolton turned to the bailiff. "Summon Miss Karnes to the witness stand," he said.

A few moments later Miss Karnes returned to the witness stand.

Mason turned to the bailiff. "I would like to have the bailiff bring Miss Della Street, my secretary, from the witness room, please."

The bailiff left the courtroom, returned a moment later with Della Street.

"Miss Karnes," Mason said, "permit me to introduce Della Street, my secretary."

"How do you do?" Miss Karnes said.

"Please look at her closely," Mason said. "Have you ever seen her before?"

"I don't think so."

"As a matter of fact," Mason said, "Miss Street was the one who bought the three ice picks from you on the evening of the second. It was Miss Street with whom you had the conversation concerning the markup in price."

Irma Karnes vehemently shook her head. "No, it wasn't!" she said. And added gratuitously, "I was told that you'd try to confuse me by running in a ringer, and I'm all prepared for that, Mr. Mason. The person who bought those three ice picks is sitting right there beside you, the defendant in this case, Mildred Crest. It was *not* Della Street who purchased those ice picks. As far as I know, I have never sold Della Street anything in my life. I am not going to permit you to confuse me by any trick substitution, Mr. Mason."

"You're absolutely positive that you never sold Miss Street anything in your life?"

"To my best recollection I have never seen her before. I am quite certain I have never sold her anything."

"And when you were making change for the ice picks which Miss Street had purchased," Mason said, "do you remember one of the ice picks rolled off the counter and fell to the floor and she stooped and picked it up?"

"That was when I was selling the ice picks to the *defendant*," the witness snapped. "She has told you about the incident, she has described it to you, and you are trying to rattle me on cross-examination. I am not going to be rattled, Mr. Mason, I know *exactly* what happened. I know that I sold these ice picks to the defendant in this case. I saw her. I recognized her, and I have studied her features too carefully to be confused."

Mason said angrily, "You've studied her features, all right, but that careful study took place when the police let you have her under observation for a full ten minutes. You didn't make that careful study of her features when she was buying the ice picks."

"I carefully studied her features when she was buying the ice picks."

"Why?" Mason asked.

"Well, because . . . because I don't intend to be confused on cross-examination, Mr. Mason."

"You didn't know you were going to be cross-examined when you were selling the ice picks," Mason said.

"Well, nevertheless, I am positive that it was the defendant who purchased the ice picks."

"And not Miss Street here?" Mason asked.

"Definitely, positively not!" Irma Karnes snapped in tones of finality. "I had been warned about you, Mr. Mason. I was prepared for this."

"Thank you," Mason said, "that's all."

"Any redirect?" Judge Bolton asked.

"No questions at all," Calvert said smiling. "You are excused from further testimony, Miss Karnes, and permit me to thank you for making an excellent witness."

Irma Karnes arose and strode from the witness stand, glowering at Mason as she passed by him.

"If the Court please," Calvert said, "that is my case. I have no further evidence which I care to put on at this time."

Mason, on his feet, said, "In that case, Your Honor, I move the Court dismiss the case against the defendant and discharge her from custody."

Judge Bolton shook his head. "The function of a preliminary examination is only to show that a crime has been committed and that there is reasonable ground for believing the defendant guilty of that crime. I think the prosecution has met that test.

"Frankly, the Court wants to hear from the defendant in this case if she wishes to avoid being bound over to the higher court for a jury trial. The testimony of the prosecution as to the actions of the defendant, if uncontradicted, discloses a background of motivation for the crime and there is at least *some* evidence tending to show the crime itself."

Mason said, "If the Court please, may I have a fifteen-minute recess? I am frank to state that I don't know whether to put the defendant on the stand and try to get the case dismissed at this time, or to sit tight, let this Court bind the defendant over for trial, and make my defense in front of a jury."

"That is a frank statement," Judge Bolton said, "and under the circumstances the Court will grant a fifteen-minute recess."

14

∎

MASON, DELLA STREET, and Paul Drake gathered for a brief conference in one of the unused witness rooms.

"Well, that's it," Mason said. "The witness Karnes saw Della Street briefly. She was led to believe that the person who bought the ice picks must have been Mildred Crest. She was given a ten-minute opportunity to study Mildred Crest. She was told that I would try to run in a ringer, her mind was conditioned against entertaining any doubt as to her opinion and—and there we are."

"So what do you do?" Drake asked.

Mason said, "I can put Della Street on the stand. She can swear that she was the one that bought the ice picks. Judge Bolton will be impressed, but in order to do any good I'm going to have to follow up by putting Mildred Crest on the stand."

"Then you'll be gambling your whole stack of chips," Paul Drake said.

Mason nodded.

"Can you afford to do that?" Paul Drake asked.

"No," Mason admitted. "However, Judge Bolton is interested now. If he has the right sort of reaction if I put Della on the stand, I'm going to go all the way. There are times when a lawyer *has* to gamble."

"Can you tell anything from Judge Bolton's facial expression?" Della Street asked.

"Not from his facial expression, but from the angle of his head. When he's interested, he leans forward. When he's decided the defendant is guilty, he leans back in his chair.

"During the examination of the last witnesses he's been leaning slightly forward. I think I'll put Della on the stand and watch the way he leans. If it's forward, I'll shoot the works.

"Come on. Let's go back to court. I want to prepare Mildred for what's to come."

They returned to court. Mason leaned over to whisper to Mildred Crest.

"Mildred," he said, "if I don't put you on the stand, the judge is going to bind you over. Then we're going to have to make our fight in front of a jury."

She nodded.

"If I put you on the stand," Mason said, "there's a chance, just a ghost of a chance, that you can convince him that there's something screwy about this case, and, while he may not turn you loose, he's pretty apt to hold that the evidence concerning deliberate first-degree murder is not sufficient to support that charge. Then he may bind you over for manslaughter."

"That will be an advantage?" she asked.

"That will be a tremendous advantage," Mason explained. "If we go to trial before a jury, some of the jurors will feel that the prosecution has proven a case of murder. One or two members will feel that you're innocent. They'll argue and discuss the case back and forth, and in the end someone will suggest as a compromise verdict that they find you guilty of manslaughter and that's what they're very apt to do.

"But once we take the murder element out of the case, and you're on trial only for manslaughter, then there's not much chance of a compromise, and the jurors who think you are innocent may hold out and get a mistrial."

"You don't seem to think too much of my chances of acquittal," she said.

"I'm talking about the worst that can happen," Mason said. "I'm painting the gloomy side of the picture for you. Now then, what do you want to do?"

"Whatever you tell me to do."

"I'm inclined to put you on the witness stand," Mason said, "but I warn you that it's going to be something of an ordeal."

"I'll tell the truth," she said.

"All right," Mason said, "here's the judge coming into the courtroom. Sit tight. Hold onto your chair. Here we go!"

15

JUDGE BOLTON CALLED Court to order and said, "I note that the district attorney, Hamilton Burger, is now personally present in court."

Hamilton Burger, big-chested, arose with ponderous dignity. "May it please the Court," he said, "a situation has developed which has been communicated to me during the recess of court. It is a situation in which I take a professional as well as an official interest.

"I note that counsel, in the cross-examination of the People's witness, Irma Karnes, brought his secretary, Della Street, forward and tried to make it appear that Miss Street was the one who had bought the ice pick which is marked in evidence as People's Exhibit Number Seven.

"I am assuming that counsel does not intend to go any further with this insinuation. I have, however, talked with the witness, Miss Karnes, during the recess, and in the event Miss Street is put on the stand to testify that she bought that ice pick, I am going to conduct her cross-examination personally. I warn Miss Street and Perry Mason that I am then going to institute proceedings for perjury. It is one thing to try to confuse a witness by running in a ringer, but it is quite another thing to try to bolster up a weak case by perjured evidence. I feel that it is only fair that I should warn counsel."

Mason turned to Hamilton Burger. "Suppose it should appear that Irma Karnes was the one who was swearing falsely. Would you then prosecute *her* for perjury?"

"Irma Karnes," Hamilton Burger said with quiet emphasis, "is telling the truth. I have talked with her personally. There can be no question as to her positive identification."

Judge Bolton said, "I fail to see where this interchange between counsel affects the issue in any way as far as this Court is concerned. Mr. Mason, you will proceed to put on the defense, in case you care to introduce your defense at this time; otherwise the matter will be submitted to the Court and the Court will make its ruling, binding the defendant over."

"I am going to accept the challenge of the prosecution," Mason said. "Della Street will take the stand."

Della Street came forward and was sworn.

"I am directing your attention to the second of this month," Mason said, "and am directing your attention to the testimony of the witness Irma Karnes, as to the defendant having purchased three ice picks from her. Are you familiar, generally, with her testimony?"

"Yes," Della Street said.

"Will you describe any transaction which you had with Irma Karnes on the second of this month?"

Della Street said firmly, "I was in the apartment of Mildred Crest. I was with you. I was instructed by you to go to the Arcade Novelty and buy three ice picks identical in design and appearance with a certain ice pick which was there in the apartment.

"I went to the Arcade Novelty. I was waited on by Irma Karnes. I bought three ice picks. She told me that it had been necessary to raise the price during the evening; that if I had been earlier, I could have had them three for a dollar. While she was ringing up the sale, prior to putting them in the bag, one of the ice picks rolled and fell on the floor. I stooped and retrieved it."

"You may cross-examine," Perry Mason said.

Hamilton Burger arose ponderously. "Miss Street, you are in the employ of Perry Mason?"

"Yes, sir."

"And have been for some time?"

"Yes, sir."

"And as such are loyal and devoted to him?"

"Yes, sir."

"You have worked with him on many of his cases. It is part of your duties to be with Mr. Mason when he interviews witnesses, to take shorthand notes and keep Mr. Mason's records straight in regard to the various cases?"

"Yes, sir."

"You were with him when he interviewed Carl Harrod?"

"Yes, sir."

"I submit to you that, on the second day of this month, you did not purchase any ice picks at the Arcade Novelty Company, that you had never seen Irma Karnes until after the second of this month. I make that suggestion to you, Miss Street, as a means of giving you a last opportunity to tell the truth. You have now testified under oath and testified falsely. A record has been made of your testimony. You have now committed perjury. I am giving you one last opportunity to retract."

"My testimony is correct," Della Street said.

"That is all," Hamilton Burger announced.

Della Street glanced up at Perry Mason.

"No more questions, Miss Street," Perry Mason said.

Della with her chin high left the witness stand, a dignity in her manner which added to her stature and subtracted from that of the discomfited, savagely angry Hamilton Burger.

Mason glanced at Judge Bolton, carefully surveying the jurist's position on the bench.

"I am going to call the defendant, Mildred Crest, to the witness stand," Mason said.

A sudden, tense hush swept the courtroom.

"All right," Mason whispered to Mildred Crest, "you're

on your own now. Remember that your weapon isn't sex appeal but sincerity. Go to it!"

Mildred Crest walked slowly to the witness stand, held up her right hand, took the oath, then faced Perry Mason.

"Mildred," Perry said, "I want to get the story of what happened on the twenty-second day of last month, the telephone conversation you had with Robert Joiner. However, for the moment, before we go into that, I think you had better tell the Court about Robert Joiner. Who was he?"

"He was the man to whom I was engaged to be married," Mildred said.

"You were wearing his ring?"

"Yes."

"You had announced your engagement to your friends?"

"Yes."

"Very well. Go ahead and tell about the telephone conversation that you had on the afternoon of the twenty-second. After that, tell us everything you did on the twenty-second, as nearly as you can remember."

In a low, self-conscious voice, Mildred Crest started to talk. Gradually, as the sound of her own voice gave her a certain measure of reassurance, she raised her eyes to Judge Bolton, straightened herself somewhat, and talked more rapidly.

Mason's questions, searching and sympathetic, prompted her whenever she slowed down, until finally she had told the story of the phone call, the automobile accident, the determination to take the identity of Fern Driscoll and the resulting complications, the meeting with Carl Harrod, the ice picks which were purchased by Katherine Baylor, the subsequent visit of Mason and Della Street, and the replacement of the two missing ice picks by Della Street.

Mason turned to the prosecuting attorney.

"Cross-examine," he said.

Hamilton Burger arose with ponderous dignity. His voice seemed sympathetic, his manner restrained.

He said, "As I understand it, Miss Crest, you suffered a terrific emotional shock on the afternoon of the twenty-second."

"I did."

"You had no suspicion that your fiancé was embezzling money?"

"None whatever."

"Certainly you must have realized that he was living beyond the salary he was earning?"

"I did. Everyone in our set did. We all accepted his statement that he came from a wealthy family and was working only to learn the business."

"So when you found he was an embezzler, you didn't want to have any part of him. Is that right?"

"Yes."

"Yet," Hamilton Burger said, raising his voice slightly and introducing an element of sarcasm, "within a few short hours after you had repudiated your boy friend because of *his* dishonesty, you yourself became a thief."

"I did not," she stormed.

"No?" Hamilton Burger asked in exaggerated surprise. "I perhaps misunderstood your testimony. I thought you said you took the purse of Fern Driscoll."

"I did. But I took it for a purpose."

"What purpose?"

"Simply so I could take over her identity until I had found myself."

"That was the only reason you had for taking her purse?"

"Yes."

"But there was four thousand dollars in her purse. Did you need that four thousand dollars in order to establish your identity as that of Fern Driscoll?"

"No."

"Yet you took that money?"

"It was in the purse."

"Oh! *It was in the purse*," Hamilton Burger said, mimicking her voice. "Is it in the purse now?"

"No."

"Who took it out?"

"I did."

"And what did you do with it after you removed it?"

"I put it in an envelope, and marked on the envelope, 'Property of Fern Driscoll.' "

"Indeed!" Hamilton Burger said. "And *when* did you do that?"

"That was before the police came to my apartment."

"Yes, yes," Hamilton Burger said smiling. "How long before?"

"Not long before."

"That was after Mr. Mason and Della Street had been there?"

"Yes."

"And didn't you write on the envelope 'Property of Fern Driscoll' at the suggestion of Mr. Mason?"

"Yes."

"That was when you knew that Carl Harrod had been stabbed in the chest with the ice pick?"

"Yes."

"In other words, all that was when you were expecting the police?"

"Yes."

"And at *that* time you put the words on the envelope, 'Property of Fern Driscoll'?"

"Yes."

"Simply as window dressing so you could assume a position of virtuous integrity when you got on the witness stand?"

"I wasn't thinking of getting on the witness stand."

"No, no, *you* weren't," Hamilton Burger said smiling,

"but your attorney was, Miss Crest. You did this at the advice of your attorney."

"I don't know what my attorney was thinking of."

"No, no, of course not. But you couldn't say that he *wasn't* thinking of a little window dressing?"

"I tell you I don't know what he was thinking."

"You followed his advice?"

"Yes."

"And up to that time you had done nothing to mark this money as being the property of Fern Driscoll?"

"I had put it to one side as her property."

"You mean you hadn't as yet spent it?"

"I had no intention of spending it."

"Did you make any effort to find out who Fern Driscoll's heirs might be?"

"No."

"Did you communicate with the Public Administrator of San Diego County where the accident took place and tell him that you had some property belonging to Fern Driscoll?"

"No."

"You say you were holding the money as the property of Fern Driscoll?"

"Yes."

"Yet you yourself were taking over Fern Driscoll's identification as well as her property?"

"I went under the name of Fern Driscoll."

"Yes, yes. You found Fern Driscoll's signature on her driving license, and you practiced signing the name of Fern Driscoll so that it would look like the signature on that driving license, didn't you?"

"Yes."

"You wrote that name on the back of a check, didn't you?"

"A check?" she asked.

"A check made out to you for your first week's wages?"

"Yes," she said, "but that was money I had earned."

"Then why did you think it was necessary for you to try to copy the signature of Fern Driscoll as it appeared on the driving license?"

"Because sometime I thought I might have to produce that driving license as a means of identification."

"You didn't know anything about Fern Driscoll's background?"

"No."

"You didn't know that she didn't perhaps have loved ones who were anxiously awaiting some word from her?"

"I knew nothing about her."

"You didn't try to communicate with her loved ones? You didn't let them know that she was dead?"

"No."

"And you deliberately set fire to the automobile so as to aid you in your deception?"

"I did not."

"The fire started as the result of a match which you had struck?"

"Yes, but it was accidental."

"You had already struck one match?"

"Yes."

"And no fire resulted?"

"That's right."

"So you tried again. You struck another match and that time a fire did result."

"I tell you the fire was accidental."

"You knew there was gasoline in the car?"

"Yes."

"You could smell it?"

"Yes."

"Notwithstanding that, you struck a match and held it over the gasoline fumes?"

"I was trying to see down into the car."

172

"And when the fumes didn't ignite, *then* you managed to drop the match so that the gasoline did ignite."

"The match burned my fingers."

"You have struck matches before?"

"Naturally."

"You know that if you hold them too long the flame will burn your fingers?"

"Yes."

"Therefore, you ordinarily blow out the match before the flame gets to your fingers?"

"Yes."

"Why didn't you do that this time?"

"I had other things on my mind."

"I certainly agree with you on that," Hamilton Burger said sarcastically.

"Now then," Hamilton Burger went on, "after Katherine Baylor had left you ice picks so that you could defend yourself in case you were assaulted, you asked her where she had bought them, didn't you?"

"Yes."

"And she told you?"

"Yes."

"So you immediately went down and bought more ice picks so that, in case you stabbed Carl Harrod with an ice pick, you could establish your innocence in the eyes of the police by showing that you still had the ice picks in your apartment that had been there when Miss Baylor had left?"

"I did not!"

"You thought that you could call on your friend Katherine Baylor and say, 'Katherine Baylor left two ice picks here, didn't you, Katherine?' and Katherine would say, 'Why, of course. Those are the ice picks that I purchased.' "

"I did not purchase any ice picks!"

"You not only took the four thousand dollars which didn't belong to you, yet don't consider yourself a thief, but you also bought three ice picks from the witness Irma Karnes, and now lie about it and presumably don't consider that you're committing perjury!"

"I didn't buy the ice picks. Della Street bought those ice picks."

"How do you know?"

"I heard Mr. Mason instruct her to buy them."

"You have heard Irma Karnes state positively that *you* purchased those ice picks?"

"She is mistaken."

"You heard her make that statement?"

"Yes."

"You heard her state that she was positive?"

"Yes."

"And still in the face of that testimony, in the face of the fact that you stabbed Carl Harrod in the chest with an ice pick which you yourself had bought from Irma Karnes, you wish to adhere to this story of your innocence, this fairy tale of having entered your apartment, of having picked up an ice pick and having some man rush at you so that he impaled his chest upon the ice pick?"

"That is the truth."

Hamilton Burger looked at the clock. "If the Court please, I think I am about finished with the witness. However, it is approaching the hour of the evening adjournment and may I ask the Court for a recess at this time with the understanding that my questioning tomorrow morning will not exceed a very few minutes?"

"Very well," Judge Bolton said. "We will continue the case until tomorrow morning at ten o'clock. The defendant is remanded to custody."

16

PERRY MASON, DELLA STREET, and Paul Drake stepped out of the elevator.

Drake said, "I'll go on to my office and see what's doing. I'll be down to your place after a while, Perry."

"Okay," Mason said. "Let me know if your men have uncovered anything important."

Mason and Della Street continued walking on down the corridor, rounded the turn and paused in front of the door marked PERRY MASON. PRIVATE.

Perry Mason fitted his latchkey, clicked back the lock, entered his private office, scaled his hat over to a chair, said, "Well, it's anybody's guess. What did you think of her, Della?"

"I think she's doing all right," Della Street said.

"Judge Bolton is watching her like a hawk."

"I know he is. He watches every move she makes, and he's leaning forward."

"And that," Mason said, "is a good sign. If he had made up his mind to bind her over, he'd simply sit there in judicial impassivity, waiting for her to get done with her testimony and then he'd announce that since there seemed to be sufficient evidence to indicate a murder had been committed, and that there was reasonable ground to believe the defendant was the guilty person, he was going to bind her over.

"You see, that mix-up on the ice picks has introduced a new note into the entire case. It means that he must consider that Mildred Crest is a deliberate, cold-blooded killer, if she did the things the prosecution claims she did."

"You mean purchasing those ice picks?" Della Street asked.

Mason nodded.

Della Street said, "I have a feeling that Judge Bolton believes me."

"I think he does, too," Mason said. "Well, I'll let Gertie know that we're back from court."

Mason picked up his telephone and, when he heard the click on the line at the switchboard, said, "We're back from court, Gertie. When you go home, fix the switchboard so outside calls come in on Della Street's telephone, will you? We're expecting—"

Gertie's voice interrupted him. She was so excited that she could hardly talk. "Just a minute! Please. . . . Hold on. . . . Just wait!" She hung up the telephone.

Mason turned to Della Street, said, "Something's got into Gertie. She's really steamed up about something."

Gertie, the incurable romanticist, came bursting into the private office, her eyes wide. "Mr. Mason, *he's* here!"

"Who?" Mason asked.

"He didn't want to give his name," Gertie went on. "He's terribly distinguished-looking, long, wavy, dark hair, that sweeps back from a beautiful forehead. Delicate features, and—"

"Who the devil are you talking about?" Mason interrupted.

"The man in the case," she said, in a hushed voice. "Forrester Baylor!"

"The devil!" Mason exclaimed.

"I don't care *what* they say, Mr. Mason. I know that he loved her. He's been living years during the past few days. The lines of suffering have etched character on his face, and—"

"Get your mind back out of the clouds," Mason said brusquely. "Send him in, Gertie, and don't go home. Stick on the switchboard. If any newspaper reporters call, lie like a trooper."

Gertie whirled with a swirl of skirts, showing a flash of well-rounded, nylon-clad legs.

"Well," Della Street said, as Gertie rushed from the office. "The plot thickens."

A moment later, Gertie was back. "Mr. Mason, Mr. Baylor," she said in a hushed voice.

The man who moved slowly past Gertie was tall, straight-backed, slim-waisted, and looked as though he hadn't slept for a week. The dark eyes seemed lackluster, although the face had breeding and character.

"Mr. Mason," he said in a low voice, and his long, strong fingers gripped the lawyer's hand.

"My confidential secretary, Miss Street," Mason said.

Forrester Baylor bowed.

"All right," Mason said, "sit down. Let's straighten out a few things. Who told you to come here?"

"No one."

"Who knows you're here?"

"No one."

"Your father?"

Forrester Baylor shook his head. "My father forbade me to leave Lansing."

"Your sister?"

"Kitty is a good egg. She'd help me out, but I don't want anyone to know I'm here."

"Where are you staying?" Mason asked. "At what hotel are you registered?"

"I'm not registered anywhere as yet. I checked my bag in a locker at the airport and took a taxi to the depot. Then I took another taxi here. I didn't want to be followed."

"You're traveling under your own name?"

"No, under an alias, and I've taken great pains to elude the newspaper reporters in Lansing."

"What do you want?"

"I want to tell you what I've found out."

"What have you found out?"

"That my father, doubtless with the best intentions in the world, was responsible for Fern's leaving. He manipulated things quietly behind the scenes so that life in the employ of his company became unbearable for her.

"I also want to tell you that Fern was a decent, straightforward, square-shooting girl. She wasn't pregnant."

"How do you know?"

"If she had been pregnant, she'd have told me. And she didn't tell me. She . . . she wasn't that kind."

Mason watched the man narrowly. "Sit down, Mr. Baylor. Make yourself comfortable. Unfortunately, it's easy to get fooled about women."

"But I'm *not* fooled about Fern Driscoll. I . . . I realize now how very, very much I loved her."

"It's a little late for that now."

"Mr. Mason, I want you to put my father on the stand."

"Why?"

"I want certain things brought out. He's the one who gave her four thousand dollars to leave Lansing."

"How do you know?"

"I know because I didn't give her that money. I know because I was getting ready to ask her to marry me, and my father knew it. My father bitterly disapproved of Fern, not as an individual, but purely because of what he felt was her lack of social position. She was a working girl, a secretary. Dad wanted me to marry an heiress.

"My father came up the hard way. He had to work for everything he got. He has known poverty. He's known snubs. And now he's come to know snobs. In fact, he's in a fair way to become one himself.

"I was interested in Carla Addis. She's clever, in a brittle, highly artificial sort of way. She's a sophisticated product of modern wealth. I'll admit there was a fascina-

178

tion there, a glitter and a glamor, and it was easy to be swept along. There were times when *I* didn't know what *I* wanted. I was badly mixed up.

"When Fern left, I suddenly realized what she meant to me. I tried to find her. I searched in vain. I thought she was still in Lansing somewhere. Then my father told me about her death, and about the autopsy and I was . . . I was crushed! I can't believe it. I can't bring myself to believe anything like that about Fern."

"Autopsies don't lie," Mason said.

Baylor shook his head. "Things just don't add up. However, that's neither here nor there. It's too late to do anything now. But I do want you to know that my father must have given her that four thousand dollars, and heaven knows what he told her in order to get her to leave."

"You don't trust your father?"

"I admire him. I'm fond of him. I love him as a father and, in a matter of this sort, I wouldn't trust him for a minute."

"What do you want *me* to do?"

"I want you to put my father on the witness stand. I want you to make him admit that he is responsible for Fern's leaving."

"And what good would that do?"

"It would establish a lot of things."

"It wouldn't help my client," Mason said. "But I'm glad you came in. I wish you'd called several days earlier. As far as that's concerned, I wish——"

He broke off as Paul Drake's code knock sounded on the door.

Mason hesitated a moment, then said to Della Street, "Let Paul Drake in."

Della opened the door.

Mason said, "Mr. Drake, this is Forrester Baylor."

Paul Drake's face promptly became a smiling, wooden mask. His eyes completely concealed any emotion.

"How are you, Mr. Baylor? Pleased to meet you," he said, shaking hands, his manner that of one who had just met a person who means only a new face and a new name.

"I'm Forrester Baylor, the son of Harriman Baylor," the young man said, apparently stung by Paul Drake's casual attitude.

"Oh, yes," Drake said. He nodded to Perry Mason. "Got some news for you, Perry."

"What about?"

"About the four thousand dollars."

"What about it?"

"It came from the Midfield National Bank in Midfield, Arkansas. The place was held up on the seventeenth by a slender, boyish-looking individual who stood in line and pushed the usual note through the cashier's window. The note said to turn over all of the hundred-dollar bills, keep the hands in sight, not press the alarm, and to wait five minutes before reporting anything. You know, the usual type of note.

"The cashier passed over forty hundred-dollar bills. At first he thought it was a young man. Now, the more he thinks of it, he believes it was a young woman in men's clothes. He never did hear the voice.

"The description matches that of Fern Driscoll."

Forrester Baylor lunged at Drake. "You lie!" he shouted. "You—"

Drake, with the ease of long practice, slipped Baylor's punch over his right shoulder.

Mason grabbed Baylor from behind, pinioned his arms to his waist. "Easy does it! Easy does it!" Mason said.

"That's a lie! That's a dirty, despicable lie! Fern Driscoll wouldn't do anything like that any more than . . . any more than you would."

Mason swung Baylor to one side, sent him spinning down into the big, overstuffed chair by the desk.

"Sit there!" he said, his voice cracking like a whip.

"Control your damned emotions! Use your head. Give us some help. I want to know about Fern Driscoll. I want a photograph."

Baylor, somewhat dazed, said, "She wouldn't! She didn't!"

"A picture!" Mason shouted at him. "Do you have a picture?"

Almost mechanically, Baylor reached in his pocket, took out a wallet and opened it. The smiling portrait of a girl peered up at them from behind a cellophane window.

Mason grabbed the wallet.

"And," Drake said, "we found Fern Driscoll's car."

"Where?" Mason asked.

"Wrecked at the bottom of a canyon between Prescott and Phoenix."

"Anyone in it?"

"No one."

"Baggage?"

"None."

"Anything else?"

"The car apparently just ran off the road, tumbled down the canyon. There's no sign anyone was injured. The driver evidently escaped."

Mason's eyes were hard. "So the car ran off the road and on the way down the driver not only escaped but dragged out her suitcase as well?"

Drake grinned. "The local authorities don't seem to have thought of that."

"What time was the bank held up at Midfield?" Mason asked.

"Ten-thirty in the morning."

Mason jerked the picture of Fern Driscoll out of Forrester Baylor's wallet. "Paul," he said. "I want you to have copies made of this picture. I want you to get a hundred men on the job. I want every newspaper to have a copy of this picture, and I want them to have the story of the bank stick-up in Midfield. You—"

Forrester Baylor came up out of the chair. Mason stiff-armed him back into the cushions.

"What's the big idea?" Drake asked.

"Never mind the idea," Mason said. "Get the hell out of here and get started before someone stops you. Cover every motel within a driving distance of three hours east and north of Midfield. Get rid of the lead and start moving. Show this picture. Get it in the press. Notify the F.B.I."

"You're playing right into the prosecution's hands," Drake protested. "You—"

Mason, still holding Forrester Baylor in the chair, half-turned toward Paul Drake. "Get started before I fire you," he said.

Forrester Baylor still struggling to get up said with low earnestness, "Mr. Mason, I'm going to kill you for this if it takes all the rest of my life to do it!"

17

JUDGE BOLTON, sitting sternly upright, looked down upon the packed courtroom.

"The Court has seen the morning papers," he said. "I am going to ask the spectators to refrain from any demonstration of any sort.

"The defendant is in court; counsel are present. The defendant was on the stand being cross-examined by Hamilton Burger. Will the defendant please resume her position on the stand."

"Just a moment," Hamilton Burger said. "I find that I have no further questions on cross-examination."

"No redirect," Mason said.

"Very well, Mr. Mason. Call your next witness," Judge Bolton said.

"I will call Mr. Harriman Baylor as my next witness," Mason said.

"What?" Hamilton Burger shouted, in sheer surprise.

"Mr. Harriman Baylor!" Mason said, raising his voice. "Mr. Baylor, will you come forward and take the stand, please?"

Baylor jumped up and said, "I know nothing whatever about this case. I am only interested because—"

"You have been called as a witness," Judge Bolton said. "You will come forward and be sworn."

Hamilton Burger said, "If the Court please, I resent any attempt on the part of Mr. Mason to try and extricate himself by seeking to involve Mr. Baylor in a matter concerning which he knows nothing. I may state that I have personally interrogated Mr. Baylor in the greatest detail, and I am satisfied he knows nothing whatever concerning the facts of *this* case. I am satisfied that he does know certain matters concerning the background of Fern Driscoll, and it may be that the prosecution will want to bring out some of those facts when the case comes to trial in the superior court. But at this time, as part of the preliminary examination, there is nothing that Mr. Baylor knows which would be of the slightest value to the defense, and I feel that he should not be called as a witness."

"The district attorney should know," Judge Bolton said, "that the defense has it in his power to call any person he wishes as a witness. Mr. Baylor will come forward and take the stand. You will have an opportunity, Mr. District Attorney, to object to any specific question as it is asked."

Baylor reluctantly came forward.

"Hold up your right hand and be sworn," Judge Bolton said.

"If the Court please," Hamilton Burger said, "Mr. Baylor is suffering from bursitis. It will be necessary for him to hold up his left hand."

"Very well, hold up your left hand and be sworn," Judge Baylor said.

"Just a moment," Mason said. "If the Court please, I object to the district attorney giving testimony in this case."

Judge Bolton looked at Mason in surprise. "The district attorney has given no testimony in this case, Mr. Mason."

"I respectfully beg to differ with the Court. The district attorney is making statements which are evidentiary in their character and are of the highest importance."

"The district attorney said that Miss Street had committed perjury," Judge Bolton said. "The Court would have rebuked the district attorney if any objection had been made at the time. However, the Court feels that the district attorney is unquestionably sincere and that his statement was made for the purpose of saving a hardworking woman from being arrested on a charge of perjury."

"I am not referring to that," Mason said. "I am referring to Mr. Burger's statement that Mr. Baylor is suffering from bursitis and therefore cannot raise his right hand."

"Why," Hamilton Burger said angrily, "I'm not giving any testimony; I am merely explaining to the Court that such is the case."

"How do you know it's the case?" Mason asked.

"Why, Mr. Baylor . . . why, Mr. Baylor has been in my office. I have talked with him in detail. He has told me all about his trouble."

Mason grinned. "It now appears, Your Honor, that the

district attorney is not only giving testimony before the Court, but that he is giving testimony which is founded purely on hearsay."

"Just what is all this leading up to?" Judge Bolton asked.

Mason said, "Under the law, a witness is required to raise his right hand and have the oath administered. If this witness refuses to raise his right hand, I demand to know why he can't raise his right hand."

Judge Bolton regarded Harriman Baylor. "You are unable to raise your right hand because of bursitis which is, I understand, a disease which affects the shoulder?"

There was a moment of silence.

"Or," Perry Mason said, "is Mr. Baylor unable to raise his right hand because of an infection in the right arm due to the wound of an ice pick?"

"An ice pick!" Judge Bolton exclaimed.

"An ice pick," Mr. Mason repeated firmly. "If the Court will notice newspaper photographs of Mr. Baylor at the time he arrived in this city, the Court will notice he is coming down the stairs from an airplane carrying his brief case in his left hand, waving his right hand in a gesture of friendly salute, presumably at the cameraman who took the picture. At that time, according to the newspaper report, he claimed he had bursitis. If that was true, it must have been in his *left* shoulder. His right hand and his right arm were unaffected. .

"Now, I would like to know why it is that he has had this sudden indisposition, in his *right* arm. I would like to have a physician examine Mr. Baylor to see whether or not there is bursitis in the *right* shoulder, and I would like to know the names of the physicians he has consulted since he has been here in this city so that we can subpoena them and find out whether the trouble with his right arm is not due to a wound inflicted by an ice pick."

Judge Bolton said, "Mr. Mason, that is a very serious

charge, a very grave accusation. I trust that you have facts with which to back it up."

"It is no more grave than the statement made by the district attorney that Mr. Baylor was unable to raise his right hand because of bursitis," Mason said. "If you want to rebuke anybody, rebuke the district attorney."

Judge Bolton flushed. "Mr. Mason, that remark borders dangerously on contempt of Court."

"I didn't mean it that way," Mason said. "I simply felt a natural resentment that any statement I made as to the cause of Mr. Baylor's injury was accepted with the gravest doubts, whereas the district attorney was permitted to give the Court the benefit of his solemn assurance, an assurance which, as it turns out, was predicated entirely on hearsay testimony, and that *he* received *no* rebuke. I would suggest, with all due respect, that the Court examine Mr. Baylor and ask him for the names of the physicians who have treated him."

"That won't be necessary," Baylor said in a low voice. "I regret that the matter has reached this stage. I have carried on the deception long enough. My conscience is bothering me and now I am faced with complete ruination. I wish to make a statement to the Court. Mr. Mason is entirely correct. The bursitis is in my *left* shoulder. The trouble with my right shoulder is due to a wound from an ice pick which was at first painful but which now has become badly infected."

Judge Bolton banged furiously with his gavel. "Order!" he shouted. "Order! There will be order in the court or I will clear the courtroom! The spectators will refrain from making any disturbance! This is a court of justice. Now be silent."

When Judge Bolton had restored order somewhat, he looked at Baylor with a puzzled frown. "This is something," he said, "that I'm afraid I don't understand."

"It is simple enough," Baylor said. "I went to the apartment of Mildred Crest because I felt that I had to have certain letters my son had sent Fern Driscoll which could cause the greatest embarrassment to my family and to my social position. I felt that those letters were in danger of becoming public property through the activities of a scandal magazine. The defendant wasn't there when I arrived. I entered her apartment by using a duplicate key which I obtained by bribing the janitor. I unscrewed the light bulbs so I could not be surprised and identified. I was searching for the letters with the aid of a flashlight, when the defendant unexpectedly returned.

"I suddenly realized the position in which I had placed myself. I felt that the only thing for me to do was to turn out my flashlight and in the dark rush past the young woman who blocked the doorway.

"I didn't want to hurt her, so I lowered my right shoulder and charged. What I didn't realize was that she had an ice pick in her hand. The ice pick was, by the momentum of my own charge, impaled in my arm near the shoulder and torn from her grasp. I ran down the stairs, and it was just as I was at the foot of the stairs, that I encountered Carl Harrod.

"Harrod apparently had been keeping an eye on the apartment house. He recognized me, turned and followed me.

"By that time I realized I was out of the frying pan and into the fire. Harrod had a camera. He got a flashlight picture as I ran to my car.

"The magazine with which Harrod had been negotiating for the story of my son's attachment would have paid many times as much for a story involving me as a housebreaker. I knew I was licked.

"Feeling that I might have a chance to buy my son's letters, I had arranged for a large sum of ready cash which I had on my person.

"I had withdrawn the ice pick and thrown it into the gutter before I made my arrangements with Harrod. I paid him ten thousand dollars in cash to help me out of my predicament. It was my only way out.

"Carl Harrod agreed to go to his apartment and call Perry Mason. He was to tell him that the defendant had stabbed *him* with the ice pick.

"Since I felt certain the defendant hadn't recognized me, and since we knew she'd call Mr. Mason and tell him she had stabbed someone, we felt Harrod's call to Mason would completely confuse the issues and give me a chance to keep out of it.

"I was to go to my suite in the hotel, shut off the telephone and refuse to see anyone. Harrod, however, was to report to me, using the name of Howley when he had performed his part of the bargain. I made arrangements so that any call from Howley would be put through at once.

"If Carl Harrod was able to convince Mr. Mason he was the one who had been stabbed, I was to give him another ten thousand dollars. I also realized there would be further payments, but at the moment I couldn't help myself.

"It was the only time in my life I had ever yielded to blackmail. This time I faced the pitiless publicity of a scandal magazine. I had no choice. Anything would have been better than that sort of publicity.

"We never expected Perry Mason would want to call a doctor to examine Harrod. We knew his client would have told him of the man who had rushed at her, of having stabbed him with the ice pick. It was my idea Harrod would claim the ice pick had penetrated his shoulder, but Harrod tried to put himself in a bargaining position by claiming he had been stabbed in the chest. That was so he could offer a settlement if Mr. Mason would turn over the letters we wanted. Harrod had my ten thousand dollars in cash, ten one-thousand-dollar bills. He knew that I would pay him another ten thousand dollars and that, if he could get those letters, I would pay him even more.

"Harrod knew that Mr. Mason would try at all costs to protect his client by keeping the matter from the police. Harrod, of course, was jubilant. He assured me he could handle Mr. Mason so Mason would, as he expressed it, be eating out of our hands. He said he had handled people of Mason's type before, that Mason couldn't be forced to do anything for himself, but that he could be made to do anything when it was a matter of protecting the interests of a client. Harrod assured me he was going to force Mr. Mason to turn over the letters we wanted. Harrod, of course, was expecting compensation for all of this, but he knew I would pay him more than the magazine would.

"I am sorry, Your Honor. I entered upon a scheme of deception and now I find myself trapped by my own chicanery."

Judge Bolton looked at the crestfallen, completely flabbergasted district attorney, then looked at Perry Mason.

"If this is the truth," Judge Bolton said, *"who* inflicted the fatal wound on Carl Harrod?"

"There was only one person, Your Honor," Mason said in a voice of quiet assurance, "who could possibly have done that. What Carl Harrod hadn't anticipated was that I would insist on calling a physician to make an independent examination.

"Harrod had no ice-pick wound, no wound of any nature when I was talking with him, but he knew after my interview that I had gone to summon a doctor. Carl Harrod, therefore, did the only thing he could. He told the young woman with whom he was living to insert an ice pick in his chest, not to insert it deep but to make a sufficient wound so that he could show a puncture mark to the doctor I was bringing, who was to make the examination.

"Nellie Elliston saw an opportunity to get the large sum of cash Carl Harrod had just acquired from Mr. Baylor. That is the only explanation that accounts for the facts. Harrod bared his chest. He instructed her to insert the ice pick an inch or two. She went to the utility drawer in the kitchen, took out an ice pick, returned to bend over Harrod, smiled down at him, and plunged the ice pick into his heart.

"Then she took the cash Harrod had acquired and fabricated an entirely spurious death scene and dying declaration. Because the district attorney was so anxious to get me involved in the case, he didn't have her submit to the rigorous tests which he would have imposed under other circumstances."

Judge Bolton looked around the courtroom, then turned back to Perry Mason. "How do you know all that, Mr. Mason?" he asked.

"Knowing that Irma Karnes was identifying the defendant, not because of the transaction at the Arcade Novelty, but because of mental suggestion and because of an image so firmly implanted in her mind by improper police methods, I knew there was only one thing that could have happened.

"And when I suddenly remembered the picture of Mr. Baylor arriving at the airport with his right hand waving a greeting, yet remembered that later on that same evening he had been forced to shake hands with his left hand, claiming a bursitis in his right shoulder, I knew what must have happened."

Judge Bolton said, "The Court noticed that, when Mr. Mason made his statement about the real reason Mr. Baylor could not raise his right hand, Miss Elliston slipped out of the courtroom. In order to dispose of the case at bar, the Court suggests that the district attorney instruct the officers to pick up Nellie Elliston for questioning. The Court might also suggest that it views with the greatest disapproval attempts to bolster the recollection of a witness who is making an identification so that she will not be shaken on cross-examination.

"The Court takes judicial cognizance of the fact that many of our miscarriages of justice are the result of mistaken identification, and suggests that, when a witness is making an identification, the witness be permitted to pick a person from a line-up under test conditions which are conducted with scrupulous fairness."

"And," Perry Mason said, "in order to keep the record straight, and in view of Mr. Baylor's statement, I now wish to call my last witness, Fern Driscoll."

"Who?" Judge Bolton snapped. And then added angrily, "Is this a trick, Mr. Mason?"

"This is not a trick," Mason said. "I wish to call Fern Driscoll as my next witness. She is waiting in the witness room. If the bailiff will please summon her, I will—"

"Order!" Judge Bolton shouted. "Order in the courtroom! I will have no more demonstrations. The spectators will remain orderly or I will clear the courtroom!"

Judge Bolton turned to Mason. "I trust, Mr. Mason," he said acidly, "that you are not attempting to impose upon the Court to obtain a dramatic effect. Having called Miss Driscoll as a witness, the Court is going to consider it as an abuse of the process of the Court unless you are able to produce that witness."

"Here she is now," Mason said.

Abruptly the courtroom became tensely quiet as a rather tall, dark-eyed, chestnut-haired, young woman walked slowly to the witness stand, held up her right hand, and was sworn.

"Your name?" Judge Bolton asked.

"Fern Driscoll," she said.

Judge Bolton glowered at Perry Mason. "Proceed!" he said.

"Would you kindly tell us what happened after you left the employ of the Baylor Manufacturing and Development Company in Lansing, Michigan?" Mason asked.

"I left there under circumstances that made me very despondent," she said. "I felt that I was no longer welcome in the organization. I started driving west with my car."

"And you picked up a hitchhiker?" Mason asked.

She nodded.

"And what happened?"

"The hitchhiker was a young woman who told me a story about being down on her luck. I guess she was. She told me she had listened to the importunities of a married man who told her that he loved her, that he was going to get a divorce and marry her. She found out that he was completely insincere, utterly ruthless, and when she went to him and told him she was in trouble, he simply laughed at her. He threw her out. She had lost her friends. She had no money."

"Go on," Mason said.

"I think," Fern Driscoll said, "the young woman was temporarily insane. She was desperate. I had a little money. She watched for an opportunity, clubbed me over the head, grabbed my purse, knocked me unconscious, and rolled me out on the road. When I regained consciousness, I found that she had taken my car, my suitcase, and all of my belongings. I reported the theft, but no one seemed particularly concerned.

"I felt certain my car would be recovered eventually. I even hoped nothing very serious would happen to the young woman who had stolen it. She was emotionally unstable and I believe temporarily insane. She had come to believe the world owed a living to both her and to her unborn child. It was quite in keeping with her emotional state for her to hold up a bank.

"No one paid any particular attention to me or made any effort to recover my property. It wasn't until the press announced that the identity of the bank robber was known and that Fern Driscoll had done the job, that the F.B.I. went into action. That organization located me within an hour.

"Needless to say, I knew nothing about the fact that I was supposed to have been murdered, or that this young woman was on trial, or that she wound up with my purse and my identification."

"Was the defendant who is here in court the young woman hitchhiker who stole your car?" Mason asked.

"Absolutely not!"

Mason turned to the popeyed Hamilton Burger and smiled. "Your witness," he said.

Burger said, "No.... no questions."

"That's my case, Your Honor," Mason said smiling.

"Do you have any further evidence?" Judge Bolton asked Hamilton Burger.

The district attorney merely shook his head.

"The case against the defendant is dismissed," Judge Bolton said. "Court's adjourned."

Fern Driscoll started to leave the witness stand, then suddenly stopped, her eyes on the tall man who was hurrying toward her.

"Forrie!" she said quietly.

Forrester Baylor didn't waste time in conversation. He simply took her in his arms, held her close to him, and made no attempt to conceal the tears which were coursing down his cheeks.

"My darling!" he said at length. "My darling . . . ! Oh, my darling . . . !"

So intent were the newspaper photographers on catching the scene, that Mason and his client were able to slip out of the courtroom.

MASON AND DELLA STREET entered the lawyer's private office.

Della Street moved close to Mason, held his arm, and he could feel her trembling.

"Chief," she said, "I'm so darned excited, and so. . . so . . . I want to cry."

Mason patted her shoulder. "Go ahead and cry."

"The look in his eyes—he really *did* love her, Chief! He really *did!* I mean he really *does!*"

"He shouldn't have let her get away," Mason said. "He was like so many men who take too much for granted."

She looked at him for a long, searching moment, then asked, "How in the world did you know she was alive?"

"When people start doing things that are definitely and decidedly out of character, you know that there's been a mistake somewhere," Mason said.

"Harriman Baylor *might* have paid money to Carl Harrod and started working with Carl Harrod, if Harrod had the letters his son had written to Fern Driscoll.

"However, Harrod didn't have those letters. I had them.

"We know that Harrod was stalemated. He couldn't sell his story without proof. He couldn't get proof until he got the letters, and he couldn't get the letters. Yet suddenly Harriman Baylor began to be very palsy-walsy with Carl Harrod.

"And as we gradually began to get the picture of Fern

Driscoll, we learned that everything in connection with her as the hitchhiker was out of character. She wasn't the sort of girl who would have been in the second month of pregnancy, who would have tried to wreck Mildred Crest's automobile. The whole thing simply didn't add together into a total.

"Then when I learned that the money in Fern Driscoll's purse had come from a bank robbery, that Fern Driscoll's car had been found wrecked where it had evidently been driven off the road, it didn't take too much brainwork to realize that the woman who had wrecked Mildred Crest's car wasn't Fern Driscoll at all. After all, we only knew she had Fern Driscoll's purse and suitcase and was using Fern Driscoll's name.

"Therefore, I felt that if we could broadcast the fact that Fern Driscoll was wanted for the robbery of a national bank, we'd probably get some fast action. Fortunately we did. Paul Drake's correspondent was able to get Fern Driscoll on a midnight plane, giving a happy solution to an otherwise puzzling case. Then, by calling Harriman Baylor to the stand, we had the whole case really buttoned up."

"But you wouldn't have ever thought of calling him unless you had known—"

"I should have known a lot sooner than I did," Mason said savagely. "I made the mistake of looking at things from the police viewpoint instead of from an objective viewpoint. I *knew* that Mildred Crest couldn't possibly have stabbed him with that ice pick which was produced in court. Therefore, either the police had to have mixed up the ice picks, or Nellie Elliston was the only person who *could* have killed Carl Harrod."

"What about Mildred Crest?" Della Street asked. "What's going to become of her?"

Mason's face became granite-hard. "Mildred Crest," he said, "is going to have a very nice job with the Baylor Manufacturing and Development Company. And Mr.

Harriman Baylor is going to see to it that she advances just as fast and just as far as her ability warrants."

Della Street looked up at him with misty eyes.

"Will you please bend over," she said, "so I can kiss you on the forehead?"

Mason regarded her with eyes that were tender. He said gently, "I'm afraid, Della, I can't bend quite that far. You won't mind if I'm a few inches short, will you?"

"Not at all," she told him.

From the
number 1
mystery writer
of all time

Erle Stanley Gardner's
PERRY MASON MYSTERIES

Available at your bookstore or use this coupon.

____THE CASE OF THE BEAUTIFUL BEGGAR	30784	2.25
____THE CASE OF THE DARING DIVORCEE	29499	1.95
____THE CASE OF THE FIERY FINGERS	30782	2.25
____THE CASE OF THE HAUNTED HUSBAND	30939	2.25
____THE CASE OF THE LAZY LOVER	30783	2.25
____THE CASE OF THE SHAPELY SHADOW	30940	2.25

BB BALLANTINE MAIL SALES
Dept. TA, 201 E. 50th St., New York, N.Y. 10022

Please send me the BALLANTINE or DEL REY BOOKS I have
checked above. I am enclosing $.......... (add 50¢ per copy to
cover postage and handling). Send check or money order — no
cash or C.O.D.'s please. Prices and numbers are subject to change
without notice.

Name_____

Address_____

City_____State_____Zip Code_____

Allow at least 4 weeks for delivery.

12   TA-32